Takano Rynn

Book Two of the Rita Series

Bianca Rowena

Bianca Watson Publishing

Rowena, Bianca
Takano Rynn (revised edition) / Bianca Rowena.–2nd ed.

Summary: Temple Girl, Rita, is destined to save the universe and Takano Rynn is desperate to find her. Only together can they defeat Master Dukath, the ruthless leader of the Ruling Order, before it's too late. Join Takano, Parrin and Beeps in their thrilling quest to find Rita and to protect the universe from the evil Master Dukath.

ISBN 978-1-9992041-3-6 (Softcover : alk, paper) / 978-1-9992041-4-3 (e-book)

[1. Sci-Fi—Fiction. 2. Fantasy.] I. Title.

Designed by Uzichu | Printed in Canada | Second Edition 10 9 8 7 6 5 4 3 2

First Published in Canada in June, 2018 by Bianca Watson Publishing

Takano Rynn / ISBN 978-0-9948513-5-2 (Softcover) / 978-0-9948513-6-9 (e-book)

*To my enigmatic friend Sheila, who is out there saving the world
from the bad guys*

contents

Takano Rynn

I CLUTCH THE MEMORY chip from the small robot, tightly in my fist. It's my only connection to Rita, these memories stored in Beeps' files. I still haven't found a compatible robot from the Opposition to install the chip into and read the files.

I lie back onto the snow and look up at the stars above Aylvon. The tree tops sway in the breeze, silhouetted by the last of the sunset as the stars take over the night sky. The wet ground seeps through my cloak and I shiver. I don't know why I came back here, to this small, abandoned planet. Maybe because it reminds me of the forest near Rita's village, where I first saw her. Maybe because this is where she found me.

Where are you, Rita? Why can't I sense you?

It's no use. She is hidden from me, hidden from Dukath. Hidden from everything and everyone by some power stronger than my own.

I can't find her. Yet, I know she's not dead.

I would have not survived it, if she were.

A shuffling noise in the dark catches my attention. I ignore it, daring anything in the forest to attack me. I could use a good fight right about now.

A memory returns. Rita walking towards me as I beckoned her with my Gift. She was so surprised when she realized what had happened, that I'd used my influence to get her to do what I wanted. She was already ahead of everyone else by realizing it had happened. Most never clued in.

We trained together here, on this planet, in this very field. She looked fragile and I was afraid to hurt her. But she was strong and quick. She was the Gift Stone I'd been searching for, and so much more. She shared the part of my life I could never share with anyone, the part that empowered me and imprisoned me at the same time. She understood.

I had made peace with the reality that I'd never be seen as a friend or a lover, or anything but the monster everyone saw me as.

Except Rita.

She insisted on looking for the good inside me, even when it wasn't there. In the end, I proved her wrong.

I'm so sorry, Rita.

I close my eyes and clench my fists.

The ground beneath me no longer feels cold but instead a burning heat against my back, like a well-deserved scourging.

It's because of me that Rita fell to the evil side of the Gift. She came to save me...

Show me where you are. I won't be afraid to love you this time.

"Rita wouldn't be happy if you died of hypothermia."

I sit up fast, sending snow flying around me.

It's the soldier, Parrin. He is standing a few yards away, already cowering like he's preparing to be stricken. I *should* strike him, the traitor. I don't understand what Rita ever saw in him as a friend. He's nothing more than a coward.

I jump to my feet, reaching for my sword, but it's gone. The vision of Rita holding my sword suddenly returns; the look on her face when she saw the dead bodies lying all around her—all those she'd killed by its blade.

"What are you doing here?" I lock Parrin in a Gift hold, angry at him for making me recall that memory.

He drops to his knees and his eyes go wide as he struggles in my choke hold. I ease off a little to let him breathe, so he can answer my question.

"I came because I knew if Rita ever returns, she'll come to you first," he says in a strangled voice.

I let him go and he falls forward, coughing.

"Who came with you?"

He rubs his neck with his hands and gives me an angry glare. I don't have to read his mind to know that he's more hurt than mad, which makes me even more annoyed at his pathetic weakness.

"Just me," he says, getting up. He's still wearing that Opposition Pilot's jacket, reminding me of when I first saw him without his Ruling Order uniform.

"I should have killed you when you first betrayed me and left the Ruling Order, *Parrin*." I put him in a hold again. I've been wanting to do this for a long time. Might as well do it now. But first, I'll search his mind.

He resists but I push past his resistance easily.

Fear is at the forefront. No surprise there.

I go deeper, into recent memories. He resists with more effort, which means he's hiding something. I find it quickly. It's shame. He's ashamed of not fighting for Rita and for letting her come after me. He's the one who told her to follow her heart and try to save me from Dukath, even when I told her to stay away.

My hold wavers for a moment at this new information. Then I tighten my grasp again.

"It's your fault she's gone now," I growl between clenched teeth. "I could kill you, here and now."

Parrin's eyes widen with fear. His mind floods with memories I don't want to see. Rita's face streaked with tears, eyes full of pain because she's worried about me. Then the pain replaced with hope as Parrin tells her to go after me, despite the heartbreak it causes him to say it. He loved her enough to let her love someone else. The concept is so foreign to me.

I loosen my hold. I'm not the only one who lost Rita that day she disappeared, he did too.

I watch through his eyes as Rita swings my sword at a girl they know as Star, a friend to both of them. This is the vision he sees in his nightmares.

I lower my arm and Parrin falls to the ground.

I shouldn't have searched his thoughts. Now I have to live with what I've seen. I didn't want to know about his love for Rita or his loyalty to his friends. It only makes me despise him more.

"How did you get away from Dukath's influence?" he asks me, his tone accusing.

I have no desire to talk to him, but I answer anyway. "He let me go. He wants me to find the sword."

"Rita has the sword. Are you going to take her to Dukath all over again?"

I lunge forward and throw Parrin against the nearest tree. His back hits the thick trunk and he cries out.

"You shouldn't have followed me here," I say, dragging him forward through the snow until he lands on his knees at my feet. He grasps at his throat again, as though trying to unlatch the invisible hold. I should kill him, for being a traitor, for standing at Rita's side like he had some kind of right to be there.

I raise him up high and throw him again, this time he hits a tree branch with the back of his head and falls into the snow. I don't have my sword to finish him off. The only thing in my hand is Beep's memory chip.

My chest tightens. Rita loved Beeps.

She also loved Parrin, as her friend.

He's unconscious now, the snow tinted red beside him. My shoulders slump and I sigh.

He's not the coward.

I am.

TarKHasH FooD

I CHECK FOR A heartbeat and sigh in relief when I find one. I've never wanted someone who I despised so much, to still be alive. If he died because of me, Rita would never forgive me. She would haunt me for the rest of my existence.

For a second, the idea is tempting.

Seeing Parrin's unconscious body lying in the snow brings back memories of my grade school friend Reagan. A memory I buried in my subconscious a lifetime ago. I killed him because of my anger. He was just a kid.

I was just a kid.

After that, I was sent away to train. Far from anyone I could harm. Far from my family, my school, my world.

I clench my fist then ram it into a tree. Bark goes flying and the pain shoots through my knuckles into my arm, making my elbow ache.

I'm my own worst enemy, not Dukath. Not the Opposition. Not the whole damn Galaxy, just... me.

Parrin coughs then turns onto his back. There's blood in his mouth.

Sorry, Rita. I just can't stand your... friend.

He blinks and looks around as though confused. I grab him by the arm and stand him up onto his feet.

"Follow me." I say, using my Gift influence on him so he'll obey.

I head for my ship and Parrin stumbles after me, having no choice but to do as I command.

* * *

I need a crew and a medic. And some servants would be nice too. I'm the strongest Gifted Master in the Galaxy and yet I'm here, attending to the wounds of an Opposition soldier.

My jaw tenses as I tighten Parrin's bandages.

"Ouch!" he cries.

I frown. Why is he so fragile?

"I'm only human you know," he says, as though answering my thought.

"So am I."

My words seem to surprise him. Did he think I was alien?

I quickly finish securing the bandage, then step away. I hate helping him. Maybe because I know he's the better man, despite his weak body. Rita would have been better off with him in the end.

I walk out of the small medic area and head for the bridge, leaving Parrin behind to tend to himself. It's time to get off Aylvon and back to looking for Rita. I'll interrogate Parrin later, when he has a little more strength. He might have some information which could help me find Rita. Maybe the Opposition has a lead, and he can tell me how far they are in their own search for her.

When I get to the bridge, I see Parrin's thoughts again. They hit me unbidden, and I have to set my hand on the wall to steady myself. The image of Rita crying for me will forever haunt me now. To Parrin, it was the moment he'd failed and I'd been victorious; the moment he realized she'd always love me and never choose him. This is the one thing in my life I somehow didn't fail at—Rita loving me despite everything.

I sigh and turn back the way I came. I need to give Parrin some water before he dies of stupidity. He lost a lot of blood and he'll need to replenish it. If I want to keep him alive long enough for Rita to see that I didn't kill him, I have to be nice.

Parrin isn't in the medic room when I get there. I go to the nearest console to search for bio-signs on board. There are two, and the one that isn't me is in the mess hall. Maybe he's not so stupid after all.

When I arrive at the mess hall, I see Parrin before he sees me. He's slouched over, resting his elbows on the table and eating something, or at least trying to. The chewy biscuit seems too hard for him to manage with the bruise across his jaw. He coughs, mid chew, then grimaces in pain.

I frown and walk over.

"That's Tarkhash food," I say just as Parrin swallows another bite. He jumps at the sound of my voice, then cringes in pain again. It takes a second for him to process what I've just said. He's already chewing another bite when the words seem to register in his brain and he spits the food out across the table.

I stifle a grin.

"Are you kidding me?" he says. "Why do you have Tarkhash food on board?"

"I'll get you something else," I say, annoyed that I'm on talking terms with one of my previous subordinates. But he's just too pathetic to be left on his own.

I walk over to the food synthesizer and push the soup and bread button. A list of options comes up, but I'm not about to ask the Traitor what he wants, so I pick a tomato-based broth.

"I've never seen one of those before," Parrin says behind me. I don't bother answering him. If he'd ever been anyone of importance in the Ruling Order, he would have had his own food synthesizer in his quarters.

I walk over to him and set the steaming hot broth down on the table.

"All I ever got was stew in the soldiers' mess hall," he continues, looking down at the soup.

"You can use the synthesizer for water too," I say, wanting the conversation to end.

Parrin nods. I pick up the energy biscuit which he'd been trying to eat earlier, to take with me to the bridge.

"I thought that was Tarkhash food," Parrin says.

I take a bit of the biscuit then turn to walk away, before he can see the grin on my face.

Parrin

"**Y**OU CAN'T JUST STICK the memory chip into the ship's system," Parrin says, coming out of nowhere.

I ignore him and continue hooking up the memory chip to the ship's main computer. It may not be a robot's body, but my ship is top of the line and can translate just about any robot language. I don't know why I didn't think to try it earlier.

"Beeps was a specialized, social robot," Parrin continues, taking a seat in the co-pilot's chair beside me. I give him a look that silences him, but likely not for long.

The small screen in the console lights up and a list of code scrolls by. I try to make sense of all the numbers but it's impossible.

"It needs to be installed into a robot body," Parrin starts up again.

"It worked," I snap.

"Yeah, but if it's in a robot like the one it came from, then she can talk to us and—"

"I don't need her to talk." I scroll through the data some more. There must be some program in the ship's database that can decode it.

"It's encrypted."

Parrin's voice grates on my nerves.

"Obviously," I grumble. "But why is it encrypted?"

"Because there's sensitive..." He trails off and doesn't and finish his sentence.

I glance over to see what's happened, but all I can gather from the look on his face is that his brain just stopped working for no apparent reason. I look back at the code. He's right; it's encrypted.

"We can take it back to the Opposition Base and..." He trails off again.

I slam my fist down on the console, making him jump. "Should I just read your mind, so we can get through this conversation faster?"

Parrin's eyes go wide and he shakes his head no.

I settle back into my seat. I have no leads in finding Rita, other than Beeps' memory chip. Maybe I could take it back to the Ruling Order Base and have them analyze it. But then

Dukath would have it, and I'm sure now that there's information on it that the Opposition doesn't want Dukath to see.

I rub at my eyes. When did I start caring about the Opposition?

"You'll take the fighter plane to the Opposition Base," I say to Parrin. "And get them to put this chip into a new robot, then bring the robot back to me."

He gets up immediately to do as I say, then stops.

"The fighter plane I came in only had enough power for a one-way trip here," he says.

I glance up. Was this some kind of suicide mission for him?

"We'll use my ship's power to recharge it—"

"And," Parrin interrupts, "I wrecked the wings in a crash landing into the trees so..."

I close my eyes for a few seconds before replying. "Then you'll tell me the location of the Opposition Base."

"What?" Parrin looks frightened. "I can't! Please don't make me."

"You'll tell me the location of your Base," I repeat, a little slower this time, using my Gift's influence on him.

"It's on Antineon," Parrin says.

Interesting.

I turn back to the console and search the ship's computer for information on the planet. Nothing comes up. I could be inputting it wrong or Parrin's pronunciation could be off, which is more likely.

I get up to give him the pilot's seat. "Then take us there."

* * *

"I just don't think it's fair you can read my mind, but I can't read yours," Parrin says.

It's the third time he's attempted to start a conversation, a different topic each time. I cross my arms and sit back in the copilot's seat. We're at quantum speed and should reach Antineon soon.

"How are we going to fly a Ruling Order Command Shuttle into the Opposition Base without getting blown out of the sky?" Parrin asks.

"Slow us down," I say, "out of Quantum Drive.

Parrin looks down at the control console with a blank stare, and doesn't do anything.

I wait.

"Over there." I point to the controls. He still can't seem to figure it out.

I lift him out of his chair so we can trade places.

"Hey!" he cries out as I plop him down into the copilot's seat.

I get into the pilot's seat and slow the ship down before it flies straight into Antineon at full speed.

"You could have just asked me to move," Parrin mumbles, rubbing his shoulder.

He's wearing that jacket again, the one I hate, and it's covering up the bandages around his ribs, which made me forget that he's hurt.

"Prepare the cloaking shields..." I begin to say, then decide to do it myself. I get up to switch places with Parrin again, since the controls I need are on his side.

"No, wait!" Parrin holds out his hand to stop me. "I can do it."

He turns on the cloaking shields and I look out the viewport at the planet in front of us. It's entirely covered in water. Did Parrin lie to me? How could this be the Opposition's Base?

"We should send a message to the General, to let him know we're coming," Parrin says.

My throat tightens and I can't seem to speak. The General... my father. How could I have forgotten?

I clench my jaw. I haven't seen him since he sent me away, when I was a child, and I don't want to see him now.

I slow the ship to a halt and set a new course.

"Where are we going?" Parrin asks.

"Somewhere else."

"But what about Beeps' chip?"

"We will find Rita some other way." I pause putting in the co-ordinates. Did I just say we?

No. That's not going to happen. Maybe I can drop Parrin off here and keep on going without him. Or better yet, I should turn him in, to the Ruling Order, and have him pay for his treason.

"This is Base Control. Please identify yourself." A voice comes over the comm unit. Either the Opposition's sensors have become more advanced, or my cloaking shields are outdated. Parrin reaches in front of me to press the comm button before I can stop him.

"General? This is Parrin. Don't fire, I'm with—"

I yank his hand off the comm button.

"Parrin?" My father's voice suddenly comes over the speakers. It's strange to hear him, after so long. He wasn't a General when I left, but I'd heard he'd become one, while I was away.

"Why is your ship cloaked?" he continues. "What ship are you flying?"

Parrin looks over at me. "Do you want to explain this to him?" he asks.

I glare at him and he turns back to the comm system.

"Um...requesting permission to land a Ruling Order Command Shuttle."

"Can you repeat that?"

"Requesting permission to land a Ruling Order Command Shuttle, on base."

"Are you the one piloting this Ruling Order Command Shuttle, Parrin?"

Parrin glances over at me again and I resist the urge to punch him.

"Yes, Sir."

"Are you under any duress?"

"No, Sir."

"Parrin." I can hear my father's exasperated sigh over the speakers. "How exactly did you obtain a Ruling Order Command Shuttle?"

Parrin clears his throat. "I have Beeps' memory chip. We're just..." He moves away from me as far as he can while still holding the comm button, then quickly adds, "Takano Rynn is with me!"

"Bryn?"

I frown at hearing my childhood name again, which brings back a flood of unwanted memories.

I clench my fists. That's not my name anymore. This whole thing was a very bad idea.

"You alright?" Parrin whispers to me.

I don't respond and he pushes the comm button again. "I'm not under duress General. Your son wants to find Rita as much as we do, and we think the memory chip might help us do that. But we haven't been able to decode it."

There is a moment of silence.

"Permission to land granted. But not on Base territory. We'll send a shuttle to you once you've landed on an island at the other side of the planet. I'm sending you the landing coordinates now."

"Yes, sir."

"Parrin, may I please talk to Bryn?"

Parrin turns to me, and I shake my head.

"Um...we're low on power, General," Parrin says. "Comm systems are shutting down! I can't hear you anymore, General... I can't—" Parrin lets go of the button.

I rub my face with my hands. "Turn off the cloaking shields," I sigh. "We would have lost power to the cloaking shields way before the comm unit quit from lack of power."

Parrin is the worst liar I've ever encountered. Even Rita could put forth a lie when needed.

Parrin's hand hovers over the controls.

He seems to have turned stupid again.

I reach across and turn off the cloaking shields myself.

"You're not going to kill your father, are you?" Parrin asks me.

I wave my hand across his face to put him into an instant sleep, and he finally shuts up.

on the outside

I LOOK OUT ACROSS the endless expanse of ocean in every direction. The wind blows cold and unforgiving at the cliff's edge where I stand and wait. Large waves rise into the air, wild and free.

I couldn't stay inside my empty ship any longer. Parrin has the memory chip now. I didn't want to give it to him, but I handed it over anyway. Someone had to take it to the Base and I'm not welcome. My father doesn't trust me. But even worse than that, he underestimates me. I could easily have the Ruling Order destroy this entire planet with one shot of their super weapon. Doesn't he realize how much power I have, if I wanted to use it?

I take in a slow breath. It's been a while now since the shuttle craft picked up Parrin to take him to the Base, somewhere on the other side of the planet. Yet the sunset persists, as though time doesn't want to move on this planet, no matter how long I wait for word as to whether they've read the chip or not.

I shiver in the cold breeze.

My father is here on this planet. I can't remember the last time we were on the same planet together.

I dreaded the thought of seeing him again, but I didn't consider that he might not want to see me. If I were my normal self I'd fly over there and kill anyone that got in my way, until I got the answers I need from that memory chip. But my father being so near makes me feel paralyzed.

There's been no communication from the Base. I at least expected Parrin to report back or send a comm message to my ship.

I'm on the outside again, left to wait and watch like when I was a kid.

I cross my arms against the chill of the wind. My dad is smarter than my mom was. I tried to tell her that Bryn was dead. That her son no longer exists. I destroyed Bryn completely when I killed all the Gifted monks in the Temple on Orusk. I became Takano Rynn that day, and that's who I am now. I tried to tell her and she didn't listen. And it cost her her life.

But my father knows. That's why he isn't coming to see me, or asking me to go see him.

I look down at the raging waters below. The tall waves slap against the cliff's edge, splashing, foaming. I can taste the ocean on my lips.

I've seen this ocean before...

No, it wasn't me who saw it, but Rita. I saw it in her thoughts. She imagined a place like this when trying to fall asleep, on lonely nights when she missed her parents. Does she sleep now? Or is she still keeping herself awake at night, wherever she is, so she won't dream?

I close my eyes, no longer able to fight the ocean of loneliness that has followed me all my life. Everything has slipped through my fingers. I had a clear mission, for a long time, to build up the Ruling Order and rule the galaxies. It drove me, fueled me.

But now that mission is not so clear.

There will never be balance and peace, as long as Dukath still exists; but is that even what I want anymore?

It's what Rita would have wanted. But I already failed. Who can defeat Dukath now, if I couldn't?

He will forever rule the galaxies with fear and intimidation, death and suffering. The same way he taught me to rule.

I look over my shoulder at my ship.

How long should I wait here?

My chest tightens. What if I never find Rita? And the Opposition doesn't either?

A memory comes flooding back before I can stop it. I told Rita that it would be better that she dies, than for her to fall to the evil side of the Gift. Did she choose to die? Why did I tell her that? She would have never become unredeemable, like me. Even in her darkest moment she still chose to do what she felt was right, for everyone else.

Maybe, I can do the same.

Parrin will be here for her when I'm gone. If she returns.

If I die, then Dukath dies too and the black sword will die with him. Then Rita will be free of his influence and can return.

A gust of wind travels up from the water below, chilling me through. I hear Rita's words which she spoke to me the first day I met. *You're a coward*. She saw into my soul and spoke the truth.

A movement in the air above me catches my attention. It's not a plane coming to get me, but a massive bird, gliding on the wind.

I'm waiting in vain. No one is coming.

The bird's wings spread wide, larger than any I have ever seen on a bird before. It cries out, the sound piercing my heart.

Rita...

I look up at the darker sky straight above. A few stars shine through.

Where are you Morlin?

Where are you Rita?

My eyes burn with unshed tears. If I let go now, I'll lose myself in the despair.

I bow my head. Maybe it is time to let go.

The bird cries out again, circling above. I throw my arms out on either side of me, letting the ice-cold wind hit my chest.

Your father is not coming, a voice in my thoughts says. *He's already lost his true son. No one is coming, nor will they ever come to you. Not even Rita. She left you and will never return again.*

They're Dukath's words. I recognize his influence over my mind more clearly now. Did I really think I was free of him? He has said nothing to me since Rita's disappearance, letting me search for her on my own. But I will never be free of him. I was a fool to think I ever would.

The sky above and waves below seem to close in on me. This will never end. For all the love Rita gave me and for all my desperation to return that love, I still never became free.

With the large bird's cries ringing in my ears, I step over the edge of the cliff and jump.

THE REAWAKENING OF BRYN

C OLD ENTERS MY VERY bones. Saltwater stings my eyes. I'm drowning in an ocean of tears, the tears of every person I've ever harmed or killed.

The weight of my boots pulls me down into the darkness below, but I don't fight my way up. The light above glistens near the top layers of the water, disappearing fast as I sink farther down.

My lungs burn. I need air. The desperation hits fast. I struggle to swim, suddenly frantic for a breath, but my muscles seize with cold and the current pushes me to and fro. My cloak and boots are too heavy. They pull me down and my strength is fading.

The light from above disappears, swallowed up by the dark abyss of the depths below.

I'll die and Dukath's reign will finally end.

Rita will be free to return.

I don't have the strength to try anymore.

You don't have the strength alone, Bryn. Let the Gift, and all those connected to it, help you. You'll have the strength together.

Where is she? Where's Rita? I plead with the voice. It's not Dukath's voice this time. Even at the moment of death, I want to know where she is.

Dizziness sets in and my head aches.

Where Rita is, you must take Dukath also.

Where the voices of the children of good and evil

Cry out from the tombs of their masters.

My thoughts begin to fade, my chest bursting with the need for air. I gulp water.

Bryn is still inside of you.

Only he can access the true power of the Gift.

My son is not dead.

I try to keep from slipping into unconsciousness.

Mom?

I shouldn't be hearing her voice. Maybe I am truly dead.

Dukath's power lies only in his deceptions.

The Gift can give you freedom.

My boots land on something. Have I hit the bottom already? The ground rises up. Then for a moment I see the sea creature beneath me as it rises upward, pushing me towards the surface. I drift down onto my back, the weight of the water crushing my chest as we rise fast.

Suddenly, we break through the surface and I'm tossed high above the waves. I cough and water rushes out of my mouth before I can gasp for air. The ocean spins below me as I flip in the air, catching a glimpse of the gigantic sea creature below, returning back down into the water.

A sharp pain digs into my shoulders and I cry out. Something sharp clasps onto me tight, stopping me from my fall back down again. The pain cuts through me so strong that I almost pass out. Cold air rushes down over my head and I look up.

It's the large bird that was circling the island before I jumped. It flaps its wings downward, struggling with the effort of carrying me.

My wet clothes are a coat of ice. I cough and the spasm causes the bird's talons to dig deeper into my shoulder.

A second before I pass out, I see the majestic sunrise glisten on the horizon before me. Then, everything goes black.

* * *

"Should I get the medic again?"

Parrin's voice fades into my thoughts as I wake. My eyelids are too heavy to open and my body feel like a rock. I turn my head with effort, and my chin scratches against a wool blanket that I now realize is weighing me down. I'm uncomfortably hot and sweaty.

"No. The doctor has already done everything he can." It's my father's voice this time. "You could get more wood for the fire."

"Yes, sir."

Parrin's footsteps retreat then there's a sigh from my father. He rests a cool hand on my forehead and I open my eyes.

"Bryn?" he says.

He looks exactly how I remember him, only weaker and more tired looking. His beard is gray, with streaks of white, but his eyes are still the same, with that disappointed look in them I'd come to know so well.

"Dad..." My throat is dry and my voice cracks.

My father looks away. "You gave me a bit of a scare there," he says, his voice gruff. "I thought I'd lost you, too."

My jaw clenches but I don't reply. It was my fault he lost mom, and if I had died too, that would have been my doing as well.

I glance at his hands, wrinkled now with age. He looks smaller in his old age.

He sets a hand on my shoulder and I try to pull away, but can't.

"Parrin found you at the Temple. You would have died of hypothermia if he hadn't."

There's nothing to say. I've disappointed him once again. I can only imagine how pathetic it looks that I tried to end things.

I focus on the window at the other side of the room. The sky is still lit with the pinks and oranges of sunset. If I look at dad now, I'll truly drown in an ocean of regret, one that no sea creature or bird can save me from.

"Bryn..." Dad says again, then stops. My heart hammers in my chest. I don't want him to say anything. I don't want to think about the last time I saw him, or how he used to train with me when I was little, using sticks as swords.

Parrin walks in suddenly, his arms full of firewood, providing the distraction I need.

I turn my head to look at him.

He stops when he sees that I'm awake. "You jumped in the ocean because I told you not to get hypothermia, didn't you?" he says, shaking his head, thinking he's funny. "You knew that if anything happened to you, Rita would never forgive me. You're always trying to ruin my life."

"Why do you think I kept you alive?" I say, but Parrin doesn't seem to get it.

I try to move the blankets off of me, but they're too heavy and my arms are weak.

"Let me help you get up," dad says. I'm about to object when my mother's words come to me. *You don't have the strength alone, Bryn.*

I nod to my dad and he helps me move the blankets aside.

Parrin drops the firewood near the small fireplace in the corner of the room and hurries over to help me as well.

It takes every bit of my self-control to let him touch my back and push me into a sitting position. I look down and breathe a sigh of relief when I see that I'm still in my clothes.

"I've had some dry clothes brought in," Dad says, pointing to a pile of sand colored fabric on a nearby table. "We'll let you get changed."

He gets up from the chair at the side of my bed and turns to leave.

"Dad?" I say.

"Yes?"

The words don't seem to want to come out of my mouth. I want to tell him I'm sorry but I also don't want to forgive him yet.

A moment passes and Dad waits.

My shoulders slump and I look away.

"It's okay Br—Takano. We'll talk when you're feeling better."

"You can call me Bryn," I say quietly. When he doesn't reply I look up and see the frown on his face.

He turns to leave and Parrin follows him out of the room, glancing back at me with a curious expression Then they're gone.

* * *

I look down at the light-colored tunic I'm wearing, so much like the ones Morlin wore when he was still around and we were kids. The color makes me feel exposed, like it will draw attention to me. I put on my black belt and boots, which will probably make me stand out even more, but it's all I have.

When I'm done, I pull the hood over my head to hide my face. Hopefully it will keep people on the base from noticing me, although I can't do anything about my height. My stomach growls and I cringe at the tightness in my belly. I need to get out of this room and find some food.

I recognize the stone walls of this place and the moisture in the air. This is where Rita was when I met her in her dream. The room is cold and musty, yet I'm too hot. I turn to leave, when I notice a plate with one small chocolate dessert square on it. I reach for it and a beep startles me.

"That's Rita's!" a little robot says. It's speaking in basic robot language, which I recognize.

I step away from the square. "Beeps?"

"When Rita comes back, she will want to eat it." Beeps rolls closer, but keeps her distance.

I crouch down to her level. "You're back."

She slowly rolls a bit closer until I can reach her.

I pat her on the side of the head. She has a new robot body, with blue reflector stripes. Seeing her all shiny and new makes me smile.

She rolls back then does a little spin to show off her new look.

"Did you get your memory chip back?" I say to her.

"Yes," she beeps.

"Good, then you can help me find Rita."

She stops spinning and tilts her head to the side.

"How?"

"We'll work together."

WHERE SHE IS

"**W**HERE SHE IS, YOU must take Dukath also..."

Dad has a distant look in his eyes as he repeats what I told him, the words Mom told me when I was at the point of death.

I look around the large dining hall. It's empty except for Dad, Parrin and me. This castle-like residence once used to be a monastery for Gifted Masters. The endless sunrise through the arched windows gives no indication of what time of day it is, but it must be too early for the rest of the soldiers and crew to be awake because we're alone in the dining hall.

I glance down at my breakfast pudding, no longer feeling hungry. The sound of the wind and waves outside the open windows makes me shiver. I'm still cold from my jump into the icy waters. The chill doesn't want to leave my bones now, yet my hands are hot and clammy.

I'll have to find some fever medicine.

The flicker of a nearby torch draws my attention and I keep my eyes on it, clinging to that warmth. I'm inside the base now, safe, yet I still feel like I'm surrounded by ice cold water, being pulled down.

Beeps shifts at my side on the floor. She's been silent since we got here. The information she was hiding is now back in Opposition hands. It wasn't about Rita. I don't care about the war anymore. I only want Rita back.

I push my pudding bowl aside and reach for the hot mug of tomato soup instead. Parrin brought it to me saying, "Your favorite! Tomato soup!" I think it was supposed to be some kind of joke again. He's bad at making jokes. The soup is hardly my favorite.

Dad frowns at the diced fruit in front of him. "It's just like your mother to talk in riddles and not get to the point."

"Takano says it's a clue to finding Rita!" Beeps chimes in. I set my hand on her small head. She hasn't left my side for a second since I woke.

She tilts her head up to look at me.

"You can call me Bryn," I say to her.

She responds with a series of beeps, which translate to the equivalent of what an electronic smile would sound like. I smile back at her.

"Maybe what she meant," Parrin says, with a mouthful of food, "was that if we take Dukath to Rita, she'll destroy him."

Dad shakes his head slowly. "I get the feeling she's locked herself away in the very place we can contain Dukath too, for all eternity, without killing him nor letting him live either."

"I don't like the sounds of that," I say under my breath.

"Don't worry, we'll find her," Dad says.

He's different in his old age, not the distant and uncaring father I remember from my teen years. He actually hears what I say, and responds.

"You look different," Parrin says to me, pushing his bowl away and grabbing for a sandwich now.

"I'm wearing different clothes," I reply, in case he can't tell that's why I look different. I'm not surprised it took him this long to notice, though. He's just a simple-minded soldier after all.

"No, it's something else," he mumbles through a mouthful of food.

I ignore him and turn my attention back to Dad.

His somber face makes my chest ache. He's not the majestic and powerful man I admired and was afraid of in childhood.

"There's an old legend," he says softly, "about the waters of Antineon. Their waves can wash a person clean of his past, and can start them on a new path, a path of their own choosing. But many have died in these waters trying to do just that. The ocean is dangerous and wild. It chooses who should live and who should die."

No one speaks for a moment.

Parrin sets down his half-eaten sandwich and looks at me. "That's it! Takano, I mean Bryn, you look more washed and clean!"

***

Whispers float down the long corridor. I don't need to hear the words to know what is being said. I can see it in the Opposition soldiers' eyes, before they quickly look away and pretend they're not talking about me.

I keep my head held high as I walk down the stone halls of the Opposition Base. These people are not my friends and I don't care what they think.

Dad was right about the waters of Antineon.

I haven't felt Dukath's influence at all since I've risen from those waters, like an illness that has been washed away. Even my steps are lighter when I walk and my eye-sight clearer than before. So the whispers that would have angered me before, don't bother me now.

For once, I feel free from having to prove myself or asserting my authority. Let them stare. I'd be staring too, if I were them.

I hurry down the wide corridors, anxious to find Dad. I remembered something else Mom said to me while I was at the brink of death.

She said to take Dukath to where the voices of the children of good and evil cry out from the tombs of their Masters.

It has to be a clue that could help us find where Rita is.

Beeps zips along by my feet. She hasn't left my side and walked the old monastery grounds with me, around the edges overlooking the waters below. A couple times I thought she'd fall over the edge. Rita would no doubt appear to avenge Beep's death, and kill me right on the spot.

I see Parrin up ahead, talking to an Opposition pilot.

"Parrin!" I call to him.

They both look up and the pilot quickly walks away as I approach.

"Hey," Parrin says. "Aren't you supposed to be at the infirmary for some tests?"

"Bryn hates doctors!" Beeps announces beside me.

I need to stop telling her things.

"Have you seen my father?" I ask Parrin.

"No, but he's usually in the headquarters office." Parrin lowers his voice. "Did you hear the news? Apparently Randon is still alive and Dukath has found a way to build a super weapon stronger than the last one! But a hundred times smaller."

So, Randon is still alive. I'm not sure how to feel about that.

I look out the archway to my left, at the raging waters below. Randon must be overjoyed to be in command now. He's been trying to take my place for as long as I can remember, after we stopped being a team and became competitors instead, competing for Dukath's approval. For ultimate power.

"How reliable are these sources?"

Parrin shrugs. "Connor told me. So I'm not sure." He crouches down to Beeps. "Hey Beeps, give me five!" He holds out his hand, palm forward and Beeps extends a small knife. "Whoa!" Parrin pulls his hand away. "We will have to work on that one." He stands back up again. "So what did you want to talk to the General about?"

"I remembered something else my mother said."

"What?"

Beeps answers. "She said to take Dukath to the place where the voices of the children of good and evil cry out from the tombs of their Masters."

I cross my arms and stare down at her. I'll have to talk to her about not answering questions on my behalf.

"Take Dukath to the good and bad children?" Parrin asks. I'm surprised he was able to pick up even that much from Beeps' dialect.

"To the place where the voices of the children of good and evil cry out from the tombs of their Masters," I say.

"Wow," Parrin scratches his head. "That makes no sense at all. Come on, I'll show you where the Headquarters office is."

We start walking then Parrin stops. "Wait, did you say where their voices cry out... from the tombs?" He looks at Beeps.

"Yes," she says.

Parrin takes off running.

My heart leaps in my chest.

He knows where Rita is.

FINDING RITA

"'T his is where I found you, when you were unconscious," Parrin says as he climbs down a rope ladder into a hole in the ground.

"Down there?" I look down.

"No, up there, on the temple floor." Parrin disappears into the dark below and I hear his feet hit the bottom.

"Then why are you going down there?" My voice echoes into the open cavern below.

"Because this is where Rita heard the voices."

"I'm coming down," I say, then jump.

I land with an echoing boom and a cloud of dust billows up around me.

I blink into the dark tunnel. Parrin's already gone ahead into the strange green, luminous fog.

Beeps makes a sound above me.

I clench my jaw, wanting to stop Parrin from going ahead without me. But it doesn't matter who finds Rita first, as long as she's found.

Beeps calls out again and I reach up for her, lowering her down with my Gift ability. She rolls around in the dust when I release my hold.

"Thank you!" she says.

I can't help but be moved, knowing she's excited to find Rita too. Hopefully Parrin's hunch is correct.

"Beeps, stop moving," I say. Her movements are creating so much dust it's stinging my eyes and nose.

She freezes so fast that her body tilts forward and she almost lands on her face.

The sound of her gears finally stop and are replaced with distant voices drifting through the hollow cavern, crying, laughing, making all sorts of sounds, none of them coherent words. I listen more carefully for any voices that sound like Rita, but they're all children's voices. *The place where the voices of the children of good and evil cry out from the tombs of their Masters.*

Parrin reappears, breathing heavily. "I can't get any of the coffins open," he says. "You'll have to use your Gift powers or something."

I look down the long corridor. Numerous stone coffins run along both sides.

"Do you feel her presence here?" Parrin asks. "Can you use the Gift to call to her?"

Does he think I haven't tried?

I start to walk, listening, concentrating, trying to focus on the Gift. I sense a protection around this tomb, like a blocking of any connection through my Gift.

Rita... where are you?

Beeps crunches the ground beneath her wheels as she rolls along beside me. I walk to the end of the cave and stop.

"This one's open," I say to Parrin, looking down at the coffin. Could she have been here and left?

"That had the black sword in it," Parrin says. "Rita and I opened it."

I turn to him. "How did you open it?"

"I don't know," he shrugs. "We pushed the lid off?"

I walk over to the first closed coffin and crouch down to get a good grasp of its lid. I'll just have to open each and every one.

I push on the lid but it doesn't budge. Parrin joins me and we push together, as hard as we can.

When that doesn't work, I move Parrin aside and focus on my Gift energies, extending both my hands towards it. Weight and size don't matter with the Gift, it's all about strength of mind.

I focus hard, but the strange energy from the fog seems to hinder me. The lid still doesn't budge.

"There's a hold over it." I rub my face with my hands. "I can't break through it."

"The dust sure likes you," Parrin says.

I glance down at my hands. They're covered in so much of the dust that they glow. I curl my fingers into a fist. The energy coming from the dust, it feels familiar like... "Crystal."

"What?"

"That's amazing," I shake some of the dust off my hands.

"What is?"

"It's the same crystal mineral used to create the swords." All the swords of the Gifted masters were made of crystals found in the ancient temples. Crystals of different colors. Except for the black sword. It was forged with so many different crystals of other swords, that it turned black and has no color.

"Air is moving from over there," Beeps says.

She rolls to one of the coffins.

"From this coffin?" I rush over to have a look.

"No, it's coming from behind it."

Parrin and I exchange a glance then he jumps over the coffin and puts his hands out to the wall behind it. He leans forward and disappears into the wall.

I blink to clear my vision. Did he really just go through the stone? I jump over the coffin, too.

"Wait for me!" Beeps shrieks in high pitched tones behind me. I turn back and lift her over to the other side of the coffin.

The stone wall looks real, even up close. I hold my breath and put my hand out, then stop. What if it doesn't let me through, the way it did Parrin? If there's a spell that allows only the worthy of heart through, then I'm out of luck.

I move my hand forward and let out a sigh of relief when the illusion gives way.

"Come on, Beeps."

I step through the wall and Beeps follows.

On the other side, the air is so thick with crystal dust that I can't see very far. Beeps zooms ahead, swallowed up in the fog. She's equipped with nighttime vision and sensors that help her see through the fog.

The passageway is narrow and there's only one way to go; forward.

As I near the end, I see Parrin on his knees, trying to force the lid off an ancient coffin.

I kneel down beside him to help push. My shoulders ache from the eagle claw marks. I stop when my wounds begin to burn. I don't want the scars to reopen.

Parrin's forehead glistens with sweat from the effort.

"Stop," I tell him. "This isn't working."

He lets go with a cry of frustration, then turns around and leans back against the coffin, breathing hard. His jacket moves aside and I see blood seeping through his shirt.

"Your bandages..." I start to say and Parrin looks down. He sighs, rubbing his face with his hands.

I sit beside him and look out into the green fog in front of us. I don't sense Rita here. Could Parrin have been wrong? I close my eyes.

Mother, help me. You helped me in the water...

The response comes almost instantly.

The Gift helped you in the waters, not me.

She heard me.

"How do we get to Rita?" I whisper into the fog.

Use the Gift. Use your voice.

"My voice?"

"What?" Parrin asks, still breathing heavily.

"I need to use my voice to open it."

He gives me a questioning look. "You do? How?"

"You're both using your voices right now!" Beeps says.

I jump up and turn to face the coffin.

"Open!" I command. The shout gets swallowed up into the thick fog.

Parrin stands up too, as though to support my efforts somehow.

"I command you to open!" I yell.

There is a moment of silence. Even Beeps stops moving around for a moment. Nothing happens.

"Maybe be nicer?" Parrin says.

I glare at him. "Nicer?"

"I mean, everything doesn't have to be a command, does it?"

I hold back a sigh and try to think of a different approach. I hear my mother's words. *Use your Gift.*

"I can open it," I whisper.

Parrin gives me a sideways glance but I ignore him. I try again, louder this time. "*We* can open it."

Beeps rolls over to the coffin and pushes against the lid with her small head. Her gears grind in the dirt as she struggles to roll forward. The lid moves slightly.

Parrin and I exchange a surprised look then both set our hands to the lid and start pushing. It slides off in a cloud of crystal dust.

There, lying peacefully in the coffin and looking more beautiful than any person I've ever seen, is Rita.

Forgotten

WE FOUND HER. I don't want to look away, afraid that she'll suddenly disappear again if I do. I fight back a sudden wave of tears. We actually found her.

Parrin reaches in and I smack his hand away.

"How do we wake her?" he says quietly, cradling his smacked hand.

I look down at Rita's still frame. Her expression looks sad, eyes closed, arms crossed over her chest. Her skin glows with the dust. I feel her presence now, so strongly that it chokes the air from my lungs.

Rita... I call to her. Wake up... please.

Beeps rolls up against the side of the coffin, trying to look in, but she's too short to see over the edge.

"Maybe you have to kiss her," Parrin says. "To wake her."

"What?" I look at him. I always knew he was stupid, but I never realized to what extent.

"Or maybe I do," he mumbles. My fist flies up and he flinches, jumping back. I stop myself just before I punch him in the face. Maybe I should have just killed him on Aylvon.

"You just need to speak louder," Beeps adds with an extra loud, piercing sequence of sounds.

Rita's eyes flutter open and she looks up.

Parrin gasps and I clasp the edge of the coffin tight. I want to say something but my throat is too closed up to speak.

"Beeps?" Rita says in a scratchy voice. "Where are you?" She coughs and struggles to get up.

Parrin immediately reaches out to help her. I want to help too but I'm frozen in place.

She's alive.

She's here, in front of me.

I searched so long, but deep down I never believed I'd find her.

I swallow hard. One of the unshed tears I'd been trying so hard to hold back finally escapes and glides down my cheek. For a sickening moment, when we found her, I thought she was lying dead in the coffin. But she's okay. She's alive.

I let out a staggered breath.

"Where am I?" Rita rubs her eyes then blinks a couple of times. She looks at Parrin, whose hand is on her back, helping her sit up.

"Parrin!" she cries in excitement. Her joy at seeing him is like a dagger to my heart. She throws her arms around him, pulling him against the edge of the coffin. He grunts in pain but doesn't pull away.

I get up from the ground and step back.

"What are you doing here?" Rita says to Parrin. Tears run down her cheeks, making a trail over the green dust on her face. She hasn't noticed me yet.

I take another step back.

"How did you get here?" she asks Parrin.

Her words hang in the air. Parrin doesn't respond.

Even Beeps is silent.

She lets go of Parrin and looks around. I'm backed far enough away now, in the fog, that she doesn't see me right away.

"Why is there a glowing fog in the cave?" She looks down at the coffin. "The bathtub is..." Her expression turns fearful. "Parrin?" She tenses and her breathing becomes frantic. "What is this?"

He looks down at the coffin, too.

"It's a coffin," Beeps answers for him.

"What?" Rita scrambles to get up. "Get me out! Get me out!" she yells, reaching for Parrin. I step forward to help but then stop, afraid to reveal myself for some reason.

Parrin grimaces in pain as Rita puts her weight on him to step out of the coffin.

"What's the last thing you remember?" he asks her.

They settle onto the ground and Parrin puts his arm around her shoulders.

"I don't know." She closes her eyes for a moment. "The cave, Takano's cave... I was in the tub and... That's the last thing I remember."

I hold my breath. Her last memory was the bath she had on Aylvon? I try to think back to that moment. What happened up until then? She asked me to stay with her at night, she was crying. I held her in my arms and stayed up all night, not daring to move a muscle in case I'd wake her. I think we were upset with each other when I came back to find her in the tub. I said something rude, then I left again.

Rita covers her cheeks with both of her hands.

"Oh... I remember being in the tub."

"What?" Parrin frowns, a confused expression on his face. "A bathtub?"

Rita slides her hands over her face and mumbles into her palms. "How embarrassing."

"What is?" Parrin asks.

"Nothing." Rita lowers her hands and gets up. She wobbles a bit and Parrin quickly reaches to steady her.

"Parrin you're bleeding!" Rita's eyes go wide as she looks down at his stained shirt. "What happened?"

Parrin glances in my direction, searching for me in the mist. My jaw clenches and don't say anything.

"Bryn hurt him," Beeps says.

"Who did?" Rita turns to Beeps. "Beeps, you look different!" She kneels down to get a better look.

"I have a new body!" Beeps says. "I don't remember what happened because Bryn took my memory card."

"What!" Rita yells. Her anger makes me flinch. "Who is this Bryn? Why did he take your memory chip?"

"The Opposition fighters shot at me and I blew up."

"That's enough Beeps," I interrupt, stepping forward.

"Master Morlin!" Rita says, her frown turning to a smile. For a second I think she sees my brother somewhere behind me, but then I realize she's looking right at me.

I freeze. It's the clothes. Morlin always wore the lighter colored tunics. Suddenly Rita's smile fades and her hopeful expression is replaced with disdain. My heart sinks. She's remembering me the way I was when she first met me.

"Takano?" Rita wraps her arms around herself then looks to Parrin as though for help. "Can you please get me out of here?" she says to him. "I'm really thirsty."

"Sure." Parrin avoids looking at me as he helps Rita walk down the passageway.

***

Parrin cringes with every step as Rita leans on him for support. I keep my distance behind them, Beeps rolling along at my side. She is quiet now, since I told her not to share the details of what has happened, with Rita.

We walk in silence and Rita avoids me as we move through the catacombs towards the entrance that we came in. Maybe it's just her embarrassment, from her last memory of being in the tub. Maybe she remembers me walking in on her.

I slow my steps. Has she forgotten all we went through together? Maybe it's for the best, because now she doesn't remember how I betrayed her and how she killed Star with the black sword.

Those parts, I hope she never remembers.

Parrin and Rita stagger in front of me and I reach my hand out to catch them with my Gift strength. I lift give them a boost in their step. They both sigh in unison at the extra support. Parrin glances back and gives me a thumbs up with his free hand.

"Thanks, Parrin," Rita says, leaning her head on his shoulder. "Are you sure you're okay?"

"Yes. Just fine," he replies.

He wouldn't be fine if I weren't helping him. I'm tempted to let him fall to the ground, but then Rita won't have the support and they'll both collapse.

"What have you been up to since..." her words trail off. We've reached the entrance now and she stops to look up at the opening at the top of the ladder.

She won't be able to climb it, not with how weak her muscles must be from being inactive for so long.

I start to raise her up towards the opening and my shoulder throbs as I do. She screams and her eyes go wide and she looks around frantically.

"It's okay!" Parrin says, reaching his arms up to her. "Takano's just lifting you out."

Rita looks over at me, but doesn't say anything.

I look past her shoulder to the sunset colors in the sky outside, not wanting to look into her eyes and see the distrust there. I lift her the rest of the way and gently set her down at the top.

Parrin gives me a look, as though he wants to say something, but then seems to decide against it.

"You go ahead." I nod to the rope ladder hanging down. "I'll catch up."

THE HEART REMEMBERS

"**S**HE'S RESTING," DAD SAYS to me.

I nod and step away from Rita's door.

"Bryn?" Dad sets a hand on my shoulder. I flinch, still not used to hearing my childhood name, or being on talking terms with my father, who is currently the leader of the Opposition. "This isn't necessarily a bad thing," he says. "Now she can get to know you as Bryn and not... who you were before"

I pull my arm away. Rita already got to know me, the way I was before, and she still cared for me.

I look down at the cold, stone floor. Maybe Dad is right. Maybe it's better that she doesn't remember having feelings for me. Now I can do whatever it takes to destroy Dukath, without her trying to stop me from getting hurt. He is still looking for her and he'll find her soon enough. She'll need to be ready.

Or I need to leave, so he doesn't discover she's here.

"Is there somewhere I can go to be alone?" I say to Dad, my chest aching.

He nods. "I know just the place."

* * *

I walk into the small chapel and look up. The ceiling is collapsed and open to the sky above. Three rows of wooden pews sit beneath a large carving of a tree set in stone, at the front of the chapel.

I rest my hand on the back of a pew. It's cold to the touch. My breath puffs out into the chilly air. I look up at the open ceiling, then close my eyes.

"May the power of the Gift descend upon me and remain with me forever," I whisper. It's a chant that Master Kra'an taught me when I training with him, before Dukath got to me.

I'd forgotten about the temple chants. I used to recite them all the time to help me control my anger, whenever my temper would suddenly overtake me.

Master Kra'an was so patient with me. He taught me self-discipline and gave me a strict daily routine. I soon began to love the consistency of it, the order.

I take a deep breath of the fresh ocean air and start a new chant, trying not to think about what happened after Dukath came into my life.

"Make known to me the ways of the Gift. Teach me the Temple path, that I may follow it and live a life worthy of a Master.... Make known to me the ways of the Gift. Teach me—"

"Takano?"

I turn fast and see Rita standing at the entrance.

My breath catches. She's as alive and beautiful as ever, wearing a dark green dress which brushes the stone floor at her feet, and a brown shawl wrapped around her shoulders. Her eyes sparkle in the dim light and her the short hair is set in unruly waves around her face.

I look away, not wanting to stare.

"Can we talk?" she says softly.

I nod and takes a seat at one of the pews. I take a seat beside her and she slides down the bench to make more distance between us. I frown, keeping my gaze on the back of the pew in front of me.

"I talked to your father," she says.

I wait.

"He talked to me about... us."

My fists clench. This is none of my dad's business.

Rita clasps her fingers together on her lap, as though she's nervous.

"I'm sorry," she continues. "I don't remember everything that happened between us."

I shake my head, wanting to tell her it's not her fault and it's for the best that she doesn't remember, but I can't seem to speak.

"I don't think your dad knows all that's happened between us either," she continues. "But he knows that I loved you enough to put my life in jeopardy to save you."

I grip the bench seat on either side of me and don't reply.

Rita sighs and crosses her arms. "No one is telling me anything, actually. Even Parrin won't talk about it and he made Beeps promise not to say anything to me either."

"Where is she now?" I say. "I thought she'd be with you."

"Who?"

I glance over at Rita. "Beeps."

"Oh." She smiles and my heart leaps in my chest. "You care about her now, don't you?"

I look away.

"I do, too." She takes a deep breath. "To tell you the truth, I remember being drawn to you, when I got to Lower Central. I felt you calling to me and then I kept heading towards you, like I was on autopilot, with the co-ordinates set to you." She smiles down at her lap and her cheeks flush. "Even from as far as another planet, I could sense you." She stops and I hold my breath. "But it's not the same now," she whispers.

I bow my head.

"Takano?"

"Yes?"

"Why is my hair cut short?" Rita runs her hand across the back of her neck, her eyes filling with tears. She's asking me because no one else has told her anything.

I remember it clearly; Rita slicing off her hair with the black sword. She must have believed that cutting her hair would take her Gift away and save her from hurting anyone else in the future.

"Your power was never in your hair," I say softly. "It was just a myth." I still sense her Gift presence so strongly. I know she is not devoid of it, even if she cut her hair.

I glance at her again.

Did cutting her hair compromise her Gift abilities somehow? Is she more vulnerable now, to Dukath?

She wipes at her eyes and my heart sinks. Her hair was a symbol of her Temple upbringing and cutting it is likely considered an act of rebellion or sacrilege. She doesn't even remember doing it.

"I'm no longer a Temple Girl," she says.

"You'll always be a Temple Girl." I lift my hand to comfort her but then set it back onto the bench. I sigh, listening to the lull of the waves crashing below. There's so much she doesn't know.

"Even the Dark Masters used to be devout Temple Monks, long ago," I tell her, after a moment. "No one is holy, Rita."

An oncoming wind whistles through the cracks of the chapel, bringing with it the scent of rain. I take a deep breath. How will I tell her about Dukath and the danger she's in? Is it better if she just never knows the bad things, or the good things, that she's forgotten?

A lump forms in my throat and my eyes burn. I focus on a beam of sunlight cutting across the room in front of us.

"What were you chanting earlier?" Rita asks.

"An Ancient Temple mantra," I reply, glad for the change of subject.

"Which one? We learned many at the Temple."

I smile. "The evening chant, before sleep."

"Not so useful for someone who doesn't sleep."

I look at her. She remembers that I told her I don't sleep? Is her memory returning?

"I don't really like to sleep." She shrugs.

I let go of the cold bench I've been gripping. She doesn't remember. She was talking about herself not sleeping.

"It can be chanted as a meditation, too. And meditations can be used as a form of sleep, when there's not enough time to sleep, or when it's too dangerous to sleep."

"We were never taught that, but it makes sense." She glances down at her hands. "Do you want to chant it together? I don't want to sleep right now, even though I'm tired. I've already been asleep in a coffin for a long time apparently."

I take a second to recall the chant, then begin. "Make known to me the ways of the Gift—"

Rita repeats after me.

"Teach me the Temple path… that I may follow it and live… a life worthy of a Master."

I start again and Rita recites the chant with me.

Our voices mingle with the breeze blowing in through the cracks in the temple walls. In the distance, I hear the cry of the eagle and the rumble of thunder.

I look up at the broken ceiling, where the light beam was just moments ago. Now there's only the gray of a cloudy sky. Lightning flashes above us as we continue to chant.

She stops chanting and I do too.

"I may not remember everything," she whispers, "but I think my heart does."

She looks right at me and I can't respond.

"I just need a little time." She gets up from the bench and moves past me. The wind dies down and I hear her footsteps retreating behind me.

Then the chapel is silent once again, except for the cries of the eagle somewhere off in the distance.

I close my eyes and smile.

Her heart remembers us.

jealous

A BLOOD-CURDLING SCREAM RIPS me from a dreamless sleep.

Rita!

I throw the blankets aside and jump out of bed. The sheets tangle at my feet and I fall hard onto the ground. I kick at the fabric, cursing under my breath. When I finally have my feet under me, I run.

The screams have stopped, which worries me more than if they'd continued.

I run down the hallway of the temple's north wing sleeping chamber area, from the room I was assigned, after Rita returned. I was given the chamber farthest from her room, my father's idea. Parrin was relocated to the south wing. Farthest from both of us. My idea.

I round a corner so fast that my hand touches the marble floor as I take the turn.

My bare feet stick well enough to the smooth marble floors, keeping me from slipping.

I burst into Rita's room a moment later, ripping the entrance curtain off its rod completely.

What I see hits me like a punch to the stomach.

Parrin's arms are wrapped around Rita as she cries.

He sees me, then quickly pulls away from her.

She looks up, too. Suddenly I'm aware I'm shirtless and Rita's gaze is on me.

I clench my fists, breathing hard from the run. How did Parrin even get here before me, since his room is in a completely different wing?

A sinking feeling settles into the pit of my stomach. Was he already here, staying in the room with her?

"Takano!" Rita cries, stretching her hands out to me. I hesitate only for a second then rush over to her. She throws her arms around me and hugs me tight. I flinch, the wounds from the eagle's talons throbbing on my shoulders.

"I had a nightmare," Rita says. "It was about you."

I pull her close and try to control my racing heart, but it's impossible.

"You jumped over the side of a cliff into the ocean and," she takes a staggering breath. "And Beeps was destroyed." Her voice catches and she squeezes me tighter. "And I killed Star!"

Suddenly she lets me go, her eyes wide and full of concern. "Where's Star?" She looks to Parrin, who is now standing off to the side, in the corner of the room.

He avoids looking at her and doesn't respond.

My heart pounds in my chest. Beeps rolls back and forth on her wheels, her gears the only sound in the drafty room.

Our silence seems to answer Rita's question and she breaks down into sobs again, covering her face with her hands. My chest tightens. I want her pain to stop.

What's happened?

The voice in my head startles me. I look to the entrance and see Dad standing there in his night clothes, frowning. I'm suddenly taken back to my childhood, when my dad would talk to me using the Gift. I'd forgotten he could do that. And yet, he was never able to use the Gift.

"Is she alright?" Dad asks Parrin, when I don't respond.

Parrin nods.

"Come on Bryn. Parrin." Dad waves his hand to us. "Let's give Rita some space."

I get up but Rita grabs my arm to stop me. She looks up at me with big, teary eyes.

"Stay," she whispers.

I swallow hard, reminded of another time when she said those words to me, on Aylvon.

"Come on, Parrin," Dad's voice is soft, patient. "You too, Beeps." He ushers them out of the room through the broken curtain. I stare after them for a moment.

Rita lets go of my arm. "You don't have to stay," she says, looking away.

I take a seat on the bed. "I want to."

Her small frame trembles slightly. "It was so real. I was flying over the ocean. I think I was an eagle, the one that watches over Antineon. And I saw your ship, on an island far away from the Base. Then I flew down closer and saw you on the edge of a cliff. I tried to call out to you but I could only cry like an eagle. And you wouldn't listen. Then you stepped over the edge."

She lowers her head and I put my arms around her, pulling her onto my lap.

She curls up close, resting a warm cheek on my bare chest. Her night gown slides away from her bare legs as she tucks her knees up to nestle into my arms. I look down at her tiny feet.

"You saved me," I whisper, running my hand over her hair to comfort her. My heart aches with all the exertion it's been getting.

Rita sets a warm palm on my chest. "I watched you dro wn..." Her hand clenches into a fist and she buries her face in my neck.

"No, you flew me to the Temple," I say, gently moving her back so she will look at me. "See the scars..."

She gasps, only now seeming to notice the talon marks on my shoulders. Her eyes glisten in the torchlight, big and bright. She's never been more beautiful.

She reaches out and gently caresses the scar on my left shoulder. "I remember now," she whispers. "I remember flying you to safety. You were so heavy."

A laugh escapes me and she gives me a shy smile, then frowns again. "I dropped you off at the entrance to the tombs, so you'd know where I was. I thought you jumped over the cliff because you were sad over me. I wanted you to know I wasn't dead. I guess I knew my body was there, in the tombs, somehow." She shivers and I pull her close again.

"Ouch," she flinches and I quickly let go. "My back is..." she trails off, her cheeks flushing.

"You hurt your back?" I ask.

She shakes her head, repositioning herself on my lap and looking away. "It's nothing."

What is it Rita?

She sighs. "It's frost bite from the coffin, lying on the cold stone for so long. The medic gave me some lotion to help it heal but I can't reach my entire back, to put it on." She turns slightly as though trying to show me her back.

I reach up and slide the top of her night gown aside so I can look. The skin there is red and looks dry and cracked.

"I didn't know who to ask," Rita continues. "For help putting the lotion on."

What about Parrin?

I know immediately that I shouldn't have said that, or thought it.

Rita gives me an angry glare. She heard it.

I don't have time to feel happy that we can communicate in this way again, through thoughts, because she climbs out of my lap and pushes me away.

"Sorry." I put my hands up in surrender.

"Parrin is just a friend," she says heatedly, standing up and glaring down at me now.

"I know," I say. Then my mind betrays me and I think, *but he was spending the night in your room.*

"What?" Rita gasps.

I lower my hands. I seem to have lost all control of my thoughts. And I'm using the Gift so easily now with Rita that it happens almost involuntarily. When did that start happening?

"He did *not* spend the night here!" Rita crosses her arms. "He was guarding my room from outside, in the hall. Which, by the way, I was unaware of until I screamed from my night-mare and he showed up a second later." She tilts her chin up, looking down her nose at me, her lips set in a tight line. I hold back a smile. She's cute when she's mad, but now isn't the time to tell her that. "And I don't see why I need to explain myself to you anyway, Takano Rynn."

My shoulders slump. "You're right. You don't."

I wipe my sweaty palms on my pants.

The room is chilly and Rita's bare feet are on the cold marble floor.

"Come, sit down, please." I stand up from the bed.

She uncrosses her arms and grins, surprising me.

"You're jealous."

I frown, then walk to the entrance. "Rita?"

"Yes?"

"Call me Bryn."

She nods.

I reach up and tie the curtain back to the rod, that I tore off when I barged into the room. Once the curtain is secure and covering the entrance again, I move it aside to step out.

"Bryn...?"

I stop, the sound of my childhood name on her lips sending a rush through me.

"Yes?" I look back at her.

"Will you please help me put the lotion on my back?" She avoids my eyes, her face flushed.

I step back into the room and set the entrance curtain back down.

"Of course."

REMEMBERING

I SCOOP THE MEDICATED ointment onto my fingertips, my hands unsteady. Rita's bare back is turned to me and she's hugging her blankets to her chest. I waited outside the room while she changed into a pair of black pants. Now she's faced away from me, her back exposed and shoulders pulled up slightly as though she's afraid the cream will hurt.

"Ready?" I ask, clearing my throat.

Rita glances over her shoulder at me and nods. I set the lotion onto her skin gently and her back stiffens.

"Too cold?" I ask, pausing.

"It's fine."

I smooth the lotion over her peeling skin as carefully as I can. Her shoulders relax and then she sighs.

I take my time, getting every part of her upper back where she couldn't reach. My eyes travel down to the arch of her lower back, wishing she needed ointment there as well.

Rita tilts her head to the side, drawing my attention to her neck. Her short hair is gathered up in pins, and my pulse races as I look at her delicate shoulders. I reach for the jar of lotion again.

I've finished applying the cream but I don't want to stop touching her yet. So I take some more lotion and start over again. Rita tilts her head to the other side and I trace my fingers up to her shoulders, then to her neck. She lets out a small gasp and I quickly pull my hand away.

"You kissed me!" she says, turning abruptly, her eyes wide, then accusing.

"What?" I try to focus on what she's saying but all I can think about is that she's now facing me, and using just one hand to hold the blanket against her. She lifts her other hand up to my face and I brace myself for a slap, but instead she touches my lips gently with her fingertips.

"In a dream. You kissed me in a dream." She suddenly pulls her hand away. "And in real life, too!"

I'm about to object when she continues.

"No," she whispers. Her eyes look past me as though she's remembering. "I kissed *you*... And you kissed me back."

I look down at her lips, which are slightly parted. If we start kissing now, I won't be able to stop and she's too fragile for that right now.

"Rita…"

"Yes?" She shifts closer to me on the bed.

"You should get dressed, before you do something you'll regret."

Her eyes flash with anger.

Then, she slaps me.

* * *

"My database says female humans' actions can seem irrational, to male humans," Beeps says to me. "But, it is common to find that their actions are actually rational, despite the initial confusion."

"Did a male or female compile that report?" I ask, looking out across the Antineon horizon. Beeps swivels her little head to look up at me. I'm sitting on the bottom steps of the amphitheater and she's seated beside me. The sun warms the side of my face and I smile.

I'd almost forgotten how wonderful it is to have the sun on my face, with all the years spent traveling in space.

"The report was compiled by a team of professors—"

"There you are!" Parrin calls out, jogging over to us.

I groan. All he's been talking about lately is the gossip about Dukath's new crystal weapon and Randon still being alive. I've been too wrapped up in my own thoughts to pay much attention to the news.

"The General called an emergency meeting at the Base Headquarters Office," he says, looking way too happy about it.

I sigh and get up. He's not going away so I'm going to have to leave if I don't want to chat.

"It's an officials-only meeting," Parrin continues.

"Then why are you going?"

Parrin's grin wavers for a second then he hurries off. "Come on!" he calls back.

Beeps follows after him in a flurry of loose gravel. I take a final moment to feel the sun on my face, then get up and head for the Base Headquarters.

FAMILY

T HE HOLOGRAPHIC IMAGE OF a diamond shaped weapon floats over the meeting table where ten commanding officers are seated, along with Rita, Parrin and me.

"Thanks to Charlie's skillful scouting, we now have this visual of the new super weapon," Dad says, nodding to Charlie.

Charlie nods back. His large hands rest on the desk in front of him and he sits up straight, his expression serious.

Dad is at the head of the table, looking poised and official in his General's uniform. "We believe it uses a massive amount of Synthetic Crystals to generate an energy field, which can travel through space to its target—"

"Does it blow up planets?" Parrin interrupts. I'm still trying to figure out why he's even here.

"It slowly kills all life on a planet through radiation exposure, but leaves the planet itself unharmed."

"Why would anyone want that?" Rita asks. She looks so pretty, even when she's worried. Now I regret not letting her kiss me last night.

I look away. No, it was good I didn't. But if only I'd kept my mouth shut, then she wouldn't have slapped me, although I still can't figure out why she did.

"Bryn?" Dad asks.

"Yes?" I look up and see that everyone is staring at me. I freeze, realizing that I must have been asked something but I don't know what.

Dad frowns. "Conner asked if you know anything more about this new weapon and how it works."

I shake my head. "All I know is that Synthetic Crystals are unstable. I don't think the Ruling Order will be successful in focusing it on a particular target, at a long distance through space."

"We have to assume they have found a way." Dad turns off the holographic image and takes a seat. "Thank you, Charlie." He nods to the tall man.

I'm no longer the tallest one on base, now that Charlie's here. I don't think he realizes I'm Takano Rynn.

At least he doesn't act like it, the way the others do.

A touch on my leg makes me jump and my knee hits the table with a bang, getting everyone's attention. Rita grins and looks away. All heads turn to me and Charlie laughs out loud.

"I guess Charlie isn't the only one too tall for our tables and chairs," Dad says with a grin. Everyone laughs and I tense. But the smiles around the room are genuine. No one's laughing at me. They're laughing at Dad's comment. He clears his throat and starts talking again about the location of the new weapon.

Rita's hand stays on my knee, warming me through the fabric of my pants. She keeps her attention on the meeting. Does this mean she forgives me?

Dad starts talking about sending out more scouts before we make any decisions on the best strategy for destroying this unstable crystal weapon. But I can't concentrate, with Rita's touch heating my leg. I can't even think coherent thoughts. All I can do is hope no one asks me any more questions.

*   *   *

"Weren't you paying attention?" Parrin says to me, talking with a mouthful of food. The dining hall is busy with the noise of the evening meal. Everyone talks and laughs as though this is a party and the fate of the universe isn't in jeopardy.

I glance around the room. They're all weak and undisciplined, not strong and bred for war, like the Ruling Order army. Do they really believe they have a fighting chance against the Ruling Order?

Rita sits silently beside me at the long table. Parrin is across from us, gesturing with his hands as he speaks.

"Basically," he says, "we destroy the crystal super weapon, then lure Dukath to the catacombs somehow."

"How?" I ask.

Parrin shrugs. "We haven't figured that part out yet."

"How about," Rita says, setting down her sandwich, "we tell him that the black sword he wants so badly is in the catacombs."

Parrin dismisses her idea with a wave of his hand. "That's not a good idea."

I glare at him and he shuts his mouth.

"You're right," Rita says, frowning. "He'll just send an army to come get it and won't come himself. Plus the Opposition Base is here. We can't jeopardize the location of the base."

"Can Dukath still, you know..." Parrin waves his hand around his ear, looking at me. "Control your mind?"

"No," I say.

Rita leans against my arm and hugs it to herself like a pillow. More than a few glances turn our way from down the table, which is filled with guys. I pretend not to notice their stares, but can't help a small grin from escaping.

Beeps rolls into my leg on the floor. "You could tell Dukath that he's the only one that can get the sword out," she beeps. "Because it's his."

I rest my hand on her head. She's a smart little robot. No one else is listening to her, though. I gently pull my arm out from Rita's grasp and get up to find another chair for Beeps. I grab one from the next table and set it beside me, then lift Beeps up onto it. Now she can see us.

Her head moves back and forth looking around the table. "Thank you," she beeps.

"Hey buddy, give me five!" Parrin says, reaching out his hand.

Beeps opens one of her compartments and extends a tiny multi-utility tool with a small screwdriver, bottle opener, scissors, pliers and tiny flashlight.

Rita chuckles.

"Pardon the interruption fellas," an Opposition Officer says, stopping at our table. "Miss," he nods to Rita. "The visitor pods will be landing soon and the guests will be gathering in the amphitheater. If you're expecting someone—"

"Visitor pods?" Parrin asks.

The officer looks to me, then Rita. "Yes, well," he clears his throat. "The General sometimes brings over family members to the base before everyone goes out on a dangerous... on an important mission."

Parrin frowns.

"Do the family members come to help us with the battle?" Beeps asks, turning to face me.

"No, they don't," I tell her. I nod to the officer. "Thank you."

He nods back and leaves.

Rita pushes her plate aside and gets up. "Excuse me," she says, then runs off. Parrin stands up too, as though he wants to run after her, but he looks at me first.

"Go ahead," I say, and he runs off.

The food sits heavy in my stomach. I want to go after Rita, but somehow I don't think she'd want me to.

I'd been avoiding having a talk with my dad, but now feels like a good time as any.

I get up and Beeps stops me. "Wait for me!"

I lift her off the seat and set her on the marble floor.

"Go find Parrin and Rita," I tell her. "And make sure he doesn't kiss her."

Beeps makes a questioning beep, which I ignore.

"Go on," I say.

Her wheels roll in one place on the marble floor for a second then she whisks away in the same direction Parrin went. I'll have to talk to someone about getting her some traction tape or rubber detailing so she can get around a bit better while she's here.

The dining hall is almost empty now. Everyone has made their way out to the amphitheater to meet their family members. I head for the Base Headquarters where I know Dad probably is.

The empty halls echo with my footsteps and I think of Rita. Her parents left her behind and this family reunion is just going to be a painful reminder to her that she doesn't have a family. She waited so long for them and they never came back. That's why she's upset now.

I start walking faster. As soon as I'm done talking with Dad, I'll go find Rita and see how she's doing.

The Headquarters office is quiet when I walk in. Dad is sitting alone, his elbows resting on the conference table and forehead in his hands. He has some papers in front of him but he's not reading them.

Pride swells in my chest. He's the commander of this whole fleet of officers and Opposition fighters. But right now he looks tired and all alone. A feeling I know all too well.

I make my way over to the table. The hum of the nearby computer mainframes drowns out the sound of my steps. I want to help, so he won't have to feel alone in all this. I know how to lead an army and how to go into battle and win. I've never been afraid to be on the front lines, unlike Randon, who stays on base to watch from a safe distance while others fight his battles for him.

Dad lifts his head and looks up.

"Bryn?" He straightens his shoulders. "Have a seat." His eyes look red, as though he's been crying.

I take a seat close to him, but not right beside him.

Dad gathers his papers and sets them aside. "How are you and Rita doing?" he asks.

I open my mouth to answer but nothing comes out.

"I know you both have Gift abilities," he continues. "And I know what that means as far as relationships go." He looks me in the eyes. "I've never seen you in such," he seems to consider his words for a moment. "So changed by someone."

I run a hand through my hair. I no longer feel like talking, but to get up and just leave would be rude, so I slouch down in my seat instead.

"If it's destined to be," Dad says, "there's always a way."

I think of Mom and a lump forms in my throat. "Do you miss Mom?" The words come out before I can stop them.

Dad leans back in his seat. "I was well practiced in missing her, even before she..." He glances at me then looks ahead. "Before she died."

I realize suddenly that my hands are shaking and I quickly set them under the table.

"I wasn't thinking clearly," I start to say. How do I explain what happened? I was able to tell Rita why I killed my mother, even then it made some kind of sense to me.

But now, here in front of my dad, it's impossible to excuse what I did. I can't even look at him.

I take a deep breath but my chest is too full for any extra air. Suddenly the Headquarters office feels too small, too enclosed. Mom's gone. She's been gone a while now. This whole time I never once stopped long enough in my goal to rule the Galaxy, to feel bad about what I did; to think about how Dad must have felt. If I'd let myself think about it, I would have become broken. Or maybe I already am. Somehow Dukath made it seem like the right thing to do at the time. But once it was done, there was no taking it back. I had to move forward. I couldn't look back.

Dad gives me a sad look. "She visited me in a dream last night."

I nod but don't respond. The hum of the overhead ventilation drones on as I wait for him to continue.

"Dad?"

He blinks a few times then seems to gather his courage. "She forgives you, Bryn."

I clench my fists. I don't want to talk about this. But I know I have to find a way to say sorry, to Dad and even Morlin. The words don't want to come out of my mouth.

Dad sets his hand onto the table, as though reaching for me, but then leaves it sitting there.

"And I forgive you, too," he says, softly.

I want to tell him I'm sorry, but I don't. There's a sudden chill in the room and I shiver.

"How's Rita?" Dad says.

I clear my throat and sit up straighter. "She still doesn't remember everything."

"All in good time."

I nod, thankful for the change in subject. Does Rita even remember how to use her Gift abilities? Would it be something she would forget?

"Why don't you ever use your Gift?" I ask Dad.

He sighs and leans forward in his seat. "I never trained to be a Master. I planned to, but then we had you and Morlin, and suddenly fighting wars and intergalactic battles didn't seem all that important anymore. All I cared about was taking care of my family..."

Dad takes a deep breath, then continues. "I loved you and Morlin so much... A father's love is one of the greatest powers in the Universe. I believe that."

He pauses, as though considering his next words carefully.

"I had my Gift abilities back then, but I was untrained. They became heightened after you were born, like a protective instinct. Of course, Morlin was with us then. I was protective of him too, but with you it was different." Dad's hands clench into fists on the table.

"I killed one of your nurses," he says, not looking at me. "It was an accident. Or, I suppose it was on purpose at the time of my anger. I don't remember deciding to do it, or thinking at all. I simply used my Gift and then..." Dad's shoulders drop and he closes his eyes. "You almost got hurt as well. I'd never done anything like that before. It was a blind rage." He stops to take a breath then opens his eyes again.

"I went to talk to the Gifted Masters and they explained about attachments and why they were forbidden for Gifted Ones. It could make a Gifted person go mad." He shakes his head. "Perhaps mad isn't the right word for it. Overprotective, jealous; normal things that can come up in attachments. But normal things aren't simply normal, when you have abnormal strength."

"So you just stopped using your Gift?" I ask.

"I no longer wanted to use it."

"You got rid of your Gift abilities?"

Was such a thing possible? What could that mean for Rita and me? If we both got rid of that part of our lives, could we be together?

"Not exactly, but yes." Dad nods. "I went with Morlin to the temple on Orusk and the Masters there reflected on my situation. They agreed to put an incantation over me that would bind my Gift to a mantra. I had no access to the Gift after the incantation was put on me, other than my connection with you when we communicated through thoughts. But that was only because you were my Gifted child. So, I can't use it, not until the incantation is lifted."

"How can it be lifted?" I ask.

"Only by chanting the same mantra used to seal my abilities, three times. The only person who knows the chant is your older brother and we still haven't found him. But I don't intend on opening the door to my powers any time soon. There are other ways to win wars and fight battles."

Dad stops talking and we sit in silence for a moment, listening to the hum of the mainframe.

I set my hands back onto the table, its smooth surface feels cool against my palms. I need to ask him the question I came here to ask. It doesn't seem like the right time now, though. But when will it ever be?

"Why did you send me away?" I say, before I can change my mind. "If you felt so protective of me?"

Dad looks surprised at the question and answers right away. "To train at the Temple, like your brother did."

I keep my eyes focused on the table, fighting the urge to overturn the expensive touch-screen glass and smash it to pieces.

"Bryn... I missed you those years you were away," Dad says. I clench my jaw and don't look at him.

"It was hard to see you struggle in school." He leans towards me and I shift away. "I didn't know what else to do."

"I didn't want to leave," I say, between clenched teeth.

"I know, but the Masters thought it would be best and... I'm sorry Bryn. I should have never sent you away when you needed us the most."

My eyes and throat burn. It's all too much.

I get up from my chair and leave.

LEFT BEHIND

CHEERFUL VOICES DRIFT OVER from the amphitheater in the distance. The air is warmer today, giving the nearby sounds of chatter a festive feel, like this is a vacation planet and not an army base.

I frown, stopping at a distance from all the activity. Do I really want to join them?

I want to talk to Rita. She wasn't in her room, the chapel or the dining hall. I searched the entire Base and the only place left to look is the amphitheater, the last place I expect her to be. But it's worth a look.

I squint into the sunlight. The fog has lifted, leaving everything bathed in orange from the sun. I walk across the crumbling cobblestone and down the steps of the amphitheater, then stop before getting too close to the crowd.

The sight of wives and children is unfamiliar to me. I'm used to seeing soldiers in uniform, not women in dresses and children running around. It reminds me of my childhood, and I don't like the feeling.

The Opposition fighters and pilots have all gathered at the center of the amphitheater, talking and laughing. I'm not about to join them. They still don't trust me, and I don't blame them.

I turn back. I'll find Rita some other time.

A beeping gets my attention and I see Beeps zooming around people's feet as a little girl chases after her. The girl's curly hair bounces around her face as she runs.

Charlie is in the middle of all the commotion, his height making him stand out in the crowd. A group of kids pull him in all directions. He doesn't seem to mind, although it's hard to tell either way.

Then I spot Rita, sitting on a step beside Parrin. My chest tightens. Rita has a little boy on her lap who appears to be telling her a story, his arms swinging about. He points up at the sky and Rita widens her eyes in exaggerated amazement at what he is telling her.

Sitting on the other side of Parrin is a little girl who looks like the twin of the bouncy haired girl chasing Beeps. She swings her feet and makes hand signals as she sings a song.

Parrin joins in with the hand movements and she stops to correct him, then they continue singing again.

I stay at the edge of the amphitheater, watching them but not wanting to go over. I'm not good with kids, or songs. I'll never be part of that picture. Even if I wanted to give Rita a family, it's forbidden for two Gifted people to marry or have children together. It's too dangerous. But Parrin could give her a normal life.

Rita's eyes light up as two more kids join her.

I turn to leave again when something bumps my leg. I look down and see Beeps. The little girl who has been chasing her stops when she sees me. She gives me a curious look, then runs away.

"Bryn," Beeps says. "Will you please help me?"

It's hard to hear her beeps over all the commotion so I crouch down. "Do you need to get away from all these kids?" I ask.

"I need to go to the Eagle Starship."

"Why?"

"I have to get something for Rita."

I look over at Rita and Parrin. He is now teaching the kids a complicated handshake as Rita laughs.

"Parrin knows how to get to the Eagle Starship," I say to Beeps. "You should ask him to take you."

Rita looks in my direction and waves. I lift my hand in greeting but don't walk over.

Beeps zooms over to Parrin and a little girl throws her arms around Beeps in a hug. I stand there watching for a moment, wondering if Rita will come over to say hi, now that she's seen me, but she simply goes back to her conversation with the boy.

I wait a moment longer, then head back inside the way I came.

* * *

I don't intend to sleep, only lay down for a moment. The sun has left me drained, despite it only being a dim sunset. But before long, I drift off to sleep.

"Having fun playing house?"

My eyes fly open.

It's Randon, standing in the entrance way to my room. I reach out my hand to lock him in a Gift hold, not sure why he's here, but he simply walks over to the window, unaffected by my attempts.

I lower my arm. This isn't real. I've fallen asleep and Dukath has let Randon into my dream. Or it's Dukath himself, appearing as Randon to antagonize me.

"All this family reunion stuff," Randon continues. "It's going to make it even more enjoyable to watch them all die." He nods his head towards the window. I go over and throw the curtain aside to have a look. A bright beam of red light streaks across the sky on its way to towards us. It's still far off but moving fast.

"They can't evacuate," Randon says behind me. "The radiation from the crystals destroys all electronics and disables the shuttle pods and ships."

I turn to face him but he is no longer there and I am alone in the room again. A little girl's scream rises above the other cries now coming from outside.

"Mommy!" Her desperate cries pierce through the commotion.

I run out of the room.

On the other side of the curtain, the hallway is not there anymore but instead I step into the living space of a small house that I don't recognize. A little girl runs past me, her bare feet patting along as she hurries from one room to the next, holding a small, hand-made doll.

"Mommy? Daddy?" Her cries become frantic as she searches each room. Her hair is like Rita's and so are her eyes.

She doesn't see me as she runs to the front door. It's locked and she struggles to get it open, her small fingers fumbling with the lock. I hurry over to help her but she opens it before I can get there, and runs out into the pouring rain on the other side.

"Rita!" I call after her. It is nighttime and I can't see where she's run off to.

I hear her voice drift on the wind as she continues to call for her parents. I try to follow after her, but the rain obscures my vision. There are no lights, just darkness. My heart pounds as I turn in every direction, searching for her.

"Rita!"

There are no more cries for her parents, only the sound of rain falling over everything.

Then suddenly she comes running out from the dark, her face crumpled with sobs. She throws her arms around my waist, hugging me tight with her little arms. "They forgot me," she cries. "They're gone."

I wake with a jolt, my chest clenching so tight that it feels like a heart attack.

"There you are." Rita comes into my room, then stops when she sees my expression.

"Bryn? What's wrong?"

"I'm sorry they left you, Rita." The words rush out before I can stop them. "They shouldn't have left you behind." I clench my fists. I don't want Rita to hurt, ever.

She hurries over to me and gives me a hug.

"Are you okay?"

"No," I say, hugging her back.

"Let's get out of here," she says against my neck.

I pull back to look at her and she sits down next to me on the bed.

"Let's go somewhere else," she adds. Her eyes light up, as though she's only now coming up with this idea.

"Where would we go?" I ask.

"How about Aylvon? Just for a day or two?"

I'm too stunned to respond. She wants to go away with me?

"The visitor families are here for a whole week," she continues. "And—"

"An entire week? I frown, remembering Randon's threats in my dream and the beam of radiation in the sky, heading for Antineon. "I need to talk to my dad." I look into Rita's hopeful eyes. "Then, after I talk to him, we'll go to Aylvon. I promise."

"I want to be alone with you." Rita's expression becomes serious, then she pulls me close again. "I have a gift for you, but I want us to be alone, away from here and from everyone, when I give it to you."

I smile. "I'll get changed and go talk to my dad now. Then we'll go."

Rita stands up. "Okay. And I'll go ask Parrin if he can watch Beeps for us while we're away."

I nod, my excitement wavering just for a moment at the mention of Parrin's name.

Rita leaves and the curtain falls behind her.

She doesn't want to bring Beeps? The only reason I can think of, is that she'd be too shy to have an audience if we were to... I shake my head. *Don't get ahead of yourself, Rynn.*

I can't help but smile at the thought of Parrin being on babysitting duty while I'm alone with Rita. I guess he might as well be useful, if I'm not allowed to get rid of him.

I'll finally get time alone with Rita. And she's getting me a gift.

I hurry to put my boots on.

If she's getting me a gift, then I need to get her a gift too!

Rita's Heritage

G REEN DUST SWIRLS IN the water around me, fizzing as it slides off my skin. The gentle splashing sounds made by my movements echo off the stone walls of the ancient bathhouse, which sits at the bottom of the island.

The ocean is calmer here, on the other side of the tall pillars of rock that surround the bathhouse. The water washes up from a small beach inlet that feeds into the pool.

I glance nervously towards the archways at the other end. No one else is here at the moment, but I feel exposed, bathing in the pool, but I wanted to clean off.

Hopefully Rita won't find out where I was before I came here to wash off the glowing dust from my skin. I want keep my gift a surprise.

The crystal dust sparkles on the water's surface in the dim sunlight.

I searched in the cracks of the cave walls, for dust that had collected over time and formed into larger pieces. I thought a green crystal would a perfect stone to set in a ring, for Rita's finger.

After taking the stones that I managed to gather from the cracks, to the repair station, I asked the repair crew if they could embed them into duranium, or some other strong alloy used on spacecrafts and robots. The mechanics seemed happy enough to take on the challenge. They weren't at the amphitheater with the others, so I could only assume they had no family visiting.

I lower my head into the chilly water, needing to wash the green dust off my hair. I'm too nervous about giving Rita the ring, to care about how cold the water is. Will she think it's odd that I'm giving her a ring? What if she doesn't want to wear it? Soon we'll be alone on Aylvon together, something which only a few days ago, I would have never imagined possible. I didn't even know if she was still alive, a few days ago.

I close my eyes and listen to the water lapping around me peacefully. The symbols carved in the pillars make me wonder if this bathhouse was used as some sort of ritual cleansing place at one time, especially since the water for the baths comes straight from the ocean; the healing waters of Antineon.

I hurry to finish rinsing off the green dust. I don't need any more healing from these waters, just a quick rinse. The dust has come off my arms but I can't see my neck or face. Hopefully there will be no trace of the stuff on me once I return. I don't want Rita to know I went back down to the catacombs. She'll have too many questions.

Just as I'm about to get out of the pool, a sound startles me and I immediately sink back down into the water. I wait a moment but don't see anyone.

I hurry out of the pool and grab the towel I brought with me, then quickly wrap it around my waist.

My clothes are in a heap on the marble floor. Why didn't I think to bring a clean change of clothes before I came?

I smooth back my hair, which is now almost shoulder length when it's wet. It'll bounce back up into waves once it dries again, but I'm going to need a haircut soon.

"Takano?" Rita's voice startles me and I turn to see her rushing towards me. "Sorry, I mean Bryn."

She's breathing hard and her cheeks are flushed from the run. She's holding a communications card in her hand.

"I was looking everywhere for you!"

Her eyes travel down to the towel wrapped around my waist. "I had…" she starts to say. "I mean, I've got…" She holds up the card as thought to show me.

"Yes?" I tilt her chin up so she'll look at me. Her cheeks flush even more and she pulls away.

"Beeps found this." She waves the comm card around . "I mean, Master Kra'an gave this to her, before he died."

I flinch. "Master Kra'an? You saw him?"

"I..." Rita seems at a loss for words. "It's a long story but yes, we saw him briefly. He told me I would fall to the evil side of the Gift and, well... he gave Beeps this message card to keep safe and give to me when I was 'with child.' So she hid it on the Eagle Starship, and today, she gave it to me."

My breath catches. With *child?* If she's pregnant with Parrin's baby I'm going to kill him. Literally.

Rita's eyes grow wide when she notices my sudden change of mood, and she quickly shakes her head, "No, Bryn. I'm not pregnant. Beeps just misunderstood what Master Kra'an meant. She saw me playing with a child today and that's why she thought I was 'with child,' like Master Kra'an had said."

I start to breathe again. Of course she wouldn't be pregnant with Parrin's baby, or anyone else's. She wouldn't be irresponsible with that sort of thing. Unless someone assaulted her... I'm glad I didn't think of that only moments ago, I would have lost my mind.

"What does the comm card say?" I ask.

"I don't know yet. I want us to watch it together." Her glance trails down again, to my towel. "Would you like me to bring you a change of clothes from your room first?"

"Please."

She nods and hurries away.

* * *

"Perhaps we should wait until Rita is actually with child, like the Master, Kra'an, wanted," Dad says.

We're gathered in Rita's room with Beeps, who has the communications card plugged in and ready to view.

Rita doesn't say anything. I put my hand on her shoulder, not sure what to tell her.

It makes sense that Kra'an would know of her. She was one of the Gifted few, and he could see visions into the future.

"Do you want me to play the message?" Beeps asks.

"Yes," Rita says. "I want to hear it."

Beeps projects a small holographic image onto the floor, in the middle of our little group.

Kra'an appears, no taller than Beeps herself. His cloak sways as he turns and my chest tightens. It's been a long time since I've seen him and the memories come flooding back. He was the one who saved me from self-destruction.

"My dearest granddaughter Rita," he begins, his holographic image gesturing towards no one in particular.

Rita gasps.

"Now you are with child and will soon find out that there are two male children in your womb."

I glance at Rita but can't tell what she's thinking. She sits perfectly still, her expression unreadable.

"One will be strong in the good side of the Gift, the other strong in the evil side. But you must not despair. They will bring balance to the Galaxy, but not without great trials and tests of character. You are a princess, my granddaughter, descended from royalty, a kingdom now long forgotten but a bloodline no less powerful. You will fulfill your destiny in your sons."

Kra'an pauses and everyone in the room seems to be holding their breath.

"Your parents were taken from you at an early age, but I hid you with an incantation so you would be unnoticed, overlooked, safe. Your true nature and power remained unseen, except by those with a pure heart. But it will be this way no longer. Soon all will see your Gift.

"You will face many trials and many sorrows, because of your sons. Take heart and remain strong. Believe in the Gift and do not give in to the evil side. Go in peace my grandchild. And may the Gift of the Masters guide you always."

The communication ends and the room is left in silence. Rita remains motionless.

Dad gets up and walks to the entranceway. He turns to look at me. "The guests will be leaving the day after tomorrow. I've cut their visit short because of the dream you told me about."

I nod.

"And," he continues, "I'd like you to return by that time, from Aylvon." He glances at Rita, then back at me. I can tell there's so much more he wants to say, but he seems to think better of it, and leaves.

AYLVON

"**W**E'RE GOING TO GET soaked!" Rita says, looking out into the downpour of rain through the spacecraft's view port. The raindrops hit the roof of the spacecraft with a loud drumming, making it hard for me to hear Rita. The season on Aylvon has changed and there is no longer snow. Instead, it's raining, the downpour muddying the ground.

"We could wait it out," I suggest.

Rita seems to consider this. She hasn't said anything about Kra'an's message on the way here and I didn't bring it up. When she's ready to talk about it, she will.

She's finally found a piece of her heritage, a family member, and now he, too, is gone.

"I don't know anything about Aylvon's seasons," she says. "This rain could last for months for all I know."

She grabs her bag and sets it onto her shoulders. "Come on. It will be an adventure!" She smiles at me and I smile back, glad that her gloomy mood has finally lifted.

"Ready?" Rita's eyes shine in the glow of the ship's auxiliary lights.

"What about the blankets and pillows?" I point towards the bed stuff, all rolled up together and tied with a rope. For a moment I expect a funny response from Beeps, but then I remember she isn't with us.

Rita snaps her fingers. "I know!" She runs off down the ship hall, without explaining.

I get the bedding and throw it onto my shoulder. My mind wanders to us wrapped up in the blankets together and I almost drop the bedding.

I have no idea what Rita has in mind for our short time away, or what she wants. Probably time to rest and relax; time away from everyone and everything. Yet with all her excitement and energy right now, I can't see us getting to sleep anytime soon.

"Here!" she returns with a large plastic bag in hand. "Now it won't get wet! Come on!" She tosses the bag to me and pushes the button for the hatch. The door opens and I quickly stuff the bedding into the bag.

The small bay area fills with the sound and scent of rain. I take a deep breath of the sweet air.

Rita gives me a wink then runs out into the downpour with a squeal.

I shake my head, but smile. Hopefully she remembers which way to go.

I grab the bag with my clothes, food and the ring in it. The mechanics did a nice job on the ring, adding carved detailing around the shining crystals embedded inside the duranium.

I brace myself for the cold rain, then run out of the ship, almost forgetting to close the bay door behind me.

The mud sticks to my boots, slowing me down as I try to hurry after Rita. The rain seeps into my cloak, cold and unrelenting. I'm already drenched and not even at the cave yet.

I try to see through the downpour. Where's Rita? She must be soaked too.

I hurry to the cave entrance and relax when I see that she is already there, waiting for me. Her arms are wrapped around herself tight, her teeth chattering.

"You need to get out of those wet clothes," I say, realizing how it sounds, only after I've said it.

Rita doesn't seem to take any offense. She grabs my arm and uses me for support as we make our way over the uneven cave floor.

The rushing sound of the rain fades away behind us and is replaced with the gentle dripping sounds of water falling into unseen puddles. Before long, it's too dark to see where we're stepping. I pull out a particle beam light from my bag and shine it down onto the cave floor.

It's covered in puddles. Hopefully the cave room doesn't have too much water in it.

We walk in silence until we reach the room. Rita has gone quiet again and I can't tell what she's thinking.

I stop at the entrance, my insides swirling with emotion. This is the place I came to recuperate, when my life was so far from where I wanted it to be, after a Temple Girl got the best of me on Green Hill. Rita stands silent beside me, as though recalling her own memories of this place.

I came here to escape Dukath's influence and to recover from being stabbed. This is where I felt the loneliest I'd ever felt in my entire life. And also where I was the most understood, accepted and loved, when Rita showed up.

I relish in her warmth against my arm as she clings onto me. I want to throw my bag and the bedding down and sweep her up into my arms. But we're almost there.

Kra'an never mentioned who the father of Rita's future children would be.

"Are you okay?" Rita asks, watching me now over the light of the particle beam. Her lips look blue with cold, but it could be a trick of the light.

I shine the light away so she won't see my face in its glare. I don't want her to even guess at what I'm thinking.

We've reached the cave room entrance and I move the light across the ground. There are puddles everywhere, trickling in-from tiny, unseen streams left unattended while I was away. I shine the light to the bed, which at least looks dry.

"We'll have to stay up there, if we want to keep dry," I say, motioning towards the bed. I groan inwardly when I realize how eager I sound to get into a bed with her. I'm not doing great with conversation on this trip.

"Let's light some candles!" Rita splashes over to the small food table and drops her bag onto it. "And start a fire."

"I'll help," I offer, but she waves me away.

"I can do it. Just go get changed. You're soaked and your cloak is dripping everywhere."

I head into the bath area, leaving Rita humming to herself as she sets up the candles. Once the curtain is drawn, I remove my belt and boots. My cloak is soaked through and heavy. A warm glow shines from beneath the curtain as candlelight fills the cave on the other side. I smile and hurry to get undressed.

I'm relieved to find that only the towels at the top of my bag got wet, and the clothes didn't.

A small box tumbles onto the floor and I quickly grab it. It's the box with Rita's ring inside. I fumble with it, almost dropping it a second time.

Should I give the ring to her now? What if she thinks it's too serious of a gesture? What if she likes me about as much as she likes Parrin? I push the thought away. It was her suggestion to come on this trip together. She's never asked Parrin to go on a trip like this alone with her, at least I hope she wouldn't.

It feels good to have my cold, wet clothes off. I want to stay shirtless, but Rita might think I'm expecting something more than what she wants, or is ready for. Or something more than *I'm* ready for.

I put on a dry pair of pants and shake the water out off my hair. I'll leave my feet bare, since they'll just get wet anyhow, on the way to the bed.

The cave is quiet now. Rita's humming has stopped. Am I taking too long?

I move the curtain aside and step out. My breath catches when I see Rita.

She's trying to pull her shirt over her head, but it's wet and stuck to her body.

I tense. I should look away. But I can't.

She finally gets the shirt over her head and tosses it across the room like a sling shot. I laugh and she notices me. Her eyes go wide and she quickly covers herself with her arms.

I brace myself for her anger. I should apologize, but I just stand there.

She doesn't say anything but walks towards me, her bare feet making tiny splash sounds as she comes.

"All the clothes in my bag got wet," she says. My pulse pounds in my ears. "Can I borrow one of your shirts?" She looks up at me from beneath her long lashes. It takes my brain a second to put an answer together.

"Yes, of course," I say, stepping aside so she can go into the bathroom. "I have more clothes in my bag."

"Thanks." She glances over her shoulder at me with a small smile before heading inside and closing the curtain.

I sit down on the bed. I need to get a hold of myself. She doesn't know I've never had any experience whatsoever with intimacy. I've seen what women look like undressed, of course, but never one as lovely as Rita.

I run my hand through my hair. I have to stop thinking about it.

The curtain opens again and I jump up in surprise.

Rita stands there with a shy smile on her face. The shirt she's put on is very large on her, reaching down to her knees and hanging off one shoulder.

"We should dry our feet and get into bed before we catch a cold," Rita says. "I still have to give you your gift."

I nod and put my hands in my pockets, so she won't see them shaking.

I Promise

RITA SITS CROSS-LEGGED, WEARING my large shirt, which is tucked into her lap. She's been quiet since we've settled onto the bed. Her cheeks are flushed and she avoids looking at me.

I stretch my legs out, leaning back against the stone wall with a pillow behind me. I could sit here forever and just look at her.

The air is warm and muggy now, from the candles, and it makes me feel sticky and sleepy. I'm too warm in my long-sleeve shirt, but I'm not sure if I should take it off or not. I don't want to make Rita uncomfortable.

She reaches up and begins to remove her hair clips. Her movements cause her shirt to slide off one shoulder. I sit up, no longer tired.

"Aren't you warm in that sweater?" she asks.

"I am." I don't need any more invitation than that. I pull my shirt over my head and toss it aside. A slight breeze blows into the cave, cooling my skin.

I sigh. Much better.

The scent of the outdoors and the forest rain wafts in with the breeze and I take a deep breath. Rita watches me with a lopsided grin on her face and I cross my arms over my chest, suddenly self-conscious.

"You were going to give me a gift?" I ask, hoping to distract her from staring at me shirtless.

Her hair is sticking out in all directions now and I resist the urge to reach out and ruffle it even more.

"I changed my mind." She shrugs and her shirt slides further down her shoulder.

"You changed your mind about giving me the gift?" I force myself to keep my gaze on her face and not her bare shoulder.

"Yes." She grabs a pillow and hugs it tight, backing away to the other side of the bed. Did I do something wrong? Is she scared of me? Should I put my shirt back on?

"I've never done anything like this before," she mumbles into her pillow. "I'm nervous."

"Oh." I nod, quite certain I know what she's talking about, but I don't want to say it out loud. It would only embarrass her more. My heart races as I try to figure out what I'm supposed to do next.

Maybe we should just relax and talk. Maybe she'd let me hold her while she fell asleep. Or maybe I'm supposed to make some kind of first move and she's waiting for me to begin. But if I do, she might slap me again.

I close my eyes and repeat a mantra in my head that the Gifted Masters taught me to say whenever I was afraid or confused. *Through the Gift, I can do all things.*

Suddenly I remember the last time I was here, on Aylvon, lying in the snow and wondering if I'd ever see Rita again.

"When you were still missing, I made a promise," I say, clutching the bed sheets in my fists. "I promised that if I ever found you again, I'd bring you back here and I wouldn't be afraid... to love you."

The room falls silent and even the drops of water seem to pause their dripping. Rita doesn't reply and I can't bring myself to look at her. I watch the shadows dance on the cave walls instead. Is she waiting for me to do something?

I swallow hard then slide over closer to her, but she immediately withdraws, her back hitting the stone wall behind her.

I tense. So she *is* scared of me.

"I won't touch you," I say, also backing away. A lump has formed in my throat and it's hard to talk, but I push past it. "You can rest." I clear my throat. "I'll go for a walk, and see if the rain has lifted yet." I get up from the bed. I can't look her in the eyes. I'm just some big brute to her; a Dark Master who killed masses of people. Why would she love a murderer?

Suddenly, Rita begins to cry and the sound pierces my heart.

"Rita?" I sit back down on the bed, but keep my distance.

"You're going to disappear too," she sobs into her pillow. "Just like my parents did."

"No—"

"If I love you, you'll leave too."

"Rita, I wouldn't."

"You left me in the interrogation chair..." she says, her breath staggered. "I remember now..."

I clench my fists. She's right. I did. She has every right to hate me, every right not to trust me. I don't even trust myself half the time.

I bow my head. "I'm so sorry." I can't break down right now. I have to be the strong one, for Rita.

"Dukath will take you from me, like he did before."

"No. Never." I move closer and put a hand on her trembling shoulder. "Rita. That will not happen. But I can understand why that would be hard for you to believe."

She lifts her head, her cheeks streaked with tears. "Can you please pass me some cloths?" She points towards her bag on the table. I jump off the bed and hurry over to it. I search inside. Her clothes are all dry and so are the cleaning cloths she's brought with her.

I can't help but grin. So they weren't went after all. Did she just want to wear one of my shirts? "Your clothes dried pretty quickly," I tease her.

She laughs behind me and it's music to my ears. I grab one of the cleaning cloths and a full sized towel, then go back to the bed.

Rita takes the cloth and wipes at her face. "Sorry," she says, her voice still shaky from crying. "I don't know what's wrong with me lately. I don't normally cry so easily."

I dry my feet with the towel then climb back onto the bed.

"Can we lay down together?" she asks.

"Yes." My shoulders relax. Some rest is exactly what we both need.

Can we lay down together, undressed? Rita says into my thoughts.

I glance over at her. Did she just say undressed?

She gives me a defiant look, her lips pursed as though she's bracing herself for my reply.

I clear my throat. "If you want to."

She turns her back to me. "You get undressed first."

I hesitate for a moment, then quickly undress and climb under the blankets to cover myself up. I lie down and pull the blanket up to my chin.

When I stop moving, she turns around and looks down at me. A smile touches her lips but is quickly replaced with a stern look. She crosses her arms, as though waiting for something.

"Oh..." I turn away from her so she can undress too. I try not to imagine her pulling her shirt over her head when I hear the rustling of cloth, but I can't help it.

A moment later, the blankets move and Rita gets under the covers behind me. I hear her soft sigh as she settles in.

Her hand touches my shoulder and my muscles instantly relax. She runs her hand down my back and I close my eyes, savoring the feel of her touch.

"I hardly remember my parents," she whispers behind me. "But I knew they were married." She stops and we lay in silence for a moment as I think about her words.

"My parents were married, too," I say softly.

I climb out of the bed, keeping covered as best I can before lowering down onto the floor to get to my pants that I tossed aside. I check the pockets.

"Bryn?" Rita says from the bed, which is too high up for her to see what I'm doing on the ground. I find the ring box and remove the ring, then grasp it tight in my fist, not wanting to drop it on the cave floor. The crystal pinches my palm.

I straighten up and kneel at the side of the bed, leaning forward on my elbows to talk to Rita. She has the blankets pulled up to her chin but I reach for her hand anyway.

"What are you doing?" she asks. I can't tell if she's afraid or curious, or both. This isn't the time to read her mind, or let her read mine.

"Rita?"

"Yes?"

I take a slow breath before continuing. How do I put this? How do I tell her everything?

"To me, we were married the moment you looked into my mind and saw my deepest and darkest fears, when we fought on Green Hill."

"Bryn..."

"You called me a coward and that's what I was." I clench the ring tighter in my hand, ignoring the burn in my palm. "I knew I'd never find anyone else like you. I knew you were the only one."

Rita sits up, lowering the blanket from her chin but still holding it close to her chest. I open my hand and the crystal glows into the dim light of the cave. Rita gasps. My heart pounds and I hold my breath.

She reaches for the ring, but I take her hand in mine before she can grab it.

"I promise I'll never leave."

She nods, her eyes glistening with tears. I slide the ring onto her finger. She smiles through her tears, lifting her hand to get a closer look.

"It's beautiful," she says. She tilts her hand to the left, then right, examining the green stones. "So that's why the mechanics wanted to measure my finger," she says. "They said it was for a new glove they were working on as a weapon for battle, but when I asked your dad about it he said he hadn't heard anything about a new battle glove."

I smile and she does, too.

"Your knees must hurt," she says. "Come back up here."

I hesitate and she raises an eyebrow.

"Here." She tosses me the towel from the bedside table then turns her back to me so I can get up without embarrassing myself.

I quickly dry my knees and feet, then climb back into bed. I catch a glimpse of her lower back when I lift the blankets to get under them and my body breaks out into a sudden heat. She turns to face me and presses her lips to mine. I don't hesitate, but reach to pull her against me and deepen the kiss, but she pulls away.

"That was my gift," she says. "I was just too nervous to give it to you earlier." She cuddles up to me and we lay down together. Her arms are tucked against her chest as she nestles into my arms. I slide my hand onto her bare back, beneath the covers. Her skin feels warm and smooth. Her breathing slows and her eyes close. She must be so exhausted after the day's events; the families arriving, the message from Kra'an, the flight to Aylvon.

I rub her back gently. The drips and drops of water all around are like little notes of music, playing at our private wedding ceremony. I lie awake, not wanting to miss a second of holding my new bride.

LIGHTNING

THE ONLY SOU IN the cave is that of Rita's breathing. Her hair falls forward, onto her flushed cheeks and her eyes are closed in concentration.

Thunder rumbles through the cave and I imagine the sky ablaze with lightning outside. Are we creating that lightning?

Rita smiles, her eyes still closed. She's so warm, so soft. I sit up and pull her against me.

I love you, I say to her with our connection.

I never want this moment to end.

Rita seems to know what she's doing, confident and unafraid. Her nails dig into my arms and suddenly she stops.

"Are you okay?"

She doesn't reply but hugs me tight. I set her hair behind her ear and try to pull back so I can see her expression, but she grips me tight.

My pulse races. Did I do something wrong? Did I hurt her?

"I'm okay," she whispers.

It's dark in the cave now. All the candles have burned out except for one. Its flame casts tall shadows on the wall behind us.

It could be the middle of the night, or early morning. I can't be sure. Rita woke me with kisses. Now her tears cool my skin.

I frown. Maybe we shouldn't have been together like this. It's too soon. There are Temple Laws which forbid such unions. What will happen now?

I close my eyes, unsure of how to reassure her. I should have been the stronger one and told her we needed to wait, to find out more about the dangers of Gifted unions. But now it's too late.

I won't let her get hurt, no matter what happens. I won't lose her again.

All of a sudden my Gift senses draw me from my thoughts. I pull away from Rita.

"What's wrong?" she asks.

"I think my dad is on his way."

"What!" Rita pulls the blanket up to her chin and looks to the cave entrance, as though my dad will appear at any second.

"He's still far off but he's definitely on his way, I can sense it."

"Are you sure?"

"Let's get dressed." I start to get up, then stop, sensing another familiar Gift connection. "And I think he's bringing Morlin with him."

Rita groans and flops back down onto the bed.

"Great timing."

IT'S TIME

The rain has stopped but the fresh scent of it still lingers in the morning air. We watch in silence as the Opposition spacecraft descends slowly towards us.

I squeeze Rita's hand. The pinch of her ring makes me smile. She didn't hate it, or give it back to me, or say that I was crazy. It symbolizes our union now, and after this morning... I quickly push the thought away. Now isn't the time to think back on our night together. Morlin and my dad are both coming to see us and I don't know why. Hopefully the vision I had about the attack on Antineon hasn't happened.

"Good thing you could tell your dad was coming, before he got here," Rita says. "Where do you think Lord Morlin's been this whole time?"

"I don't know." I watch the spacecraft approach, faster now that it's within the planet's atmosphere. "I don't think Dukath ever had him."

A rushing sound like a loud wind fills the forest as the shuttle lands in a nearby clearing. I squeeze Rita's hand again. *Are you ready for this?*

Will your dad be upset that we're... unofficially married?

It's official to me. I look down at Rita and smile.

The swaying treetops settle down after a moment and the loud sounds stop, leaving the forest in peace once again. We walk forward, our boots squishing in the fresh mud. I shift my bag on my shoulder. How do I tell my dad and Morlin that Rita and I are, as far as we're concerned, married?

Then I remember what Dad said to me, when I was little. "One day you'll find someone special, Bryn. Then this need to fit in at school, or anywhere else, won't seem to matter so much."

I never believed I'd find someone, though. I was too different, too scary to everyone. And I didn't even want to try, because I knew I'd end up hurting whomever it was, with my Gift powers.

I glance over at Rita as we make our way through the trees to the clearing where the ship is. She's strong. In many ways, stronger than me.

We stop in front of the shuttle craft and the bay doors open with a loud hissing. The ramp slowly lowers and I see my dad and Morlin standing there, stone faced and serious.

"Bryn." Dad smiles briefly and Morlin nods to us. They walk down and Dad gives me a pat on the shoulder. I turn to my brother but he doesn't offer any hellos.

He looks older, as though these last few months have aged him many years. I'd always envied him his ability to control his Gift, to meditate and know his place in the universe. He was the good son, the one that would never turn to evil. I revered him as a child, then later despised him. Now I feel neither reverence nor anger towards him. I offer my hand for a handshake and he takes it.

You're ready now, he says, pulling me into a quick hug. *You had to pass your greatest test, facing your inner battle, the hatred and desire for ultimate power. You're ready to work together with us to bring peace to the Galaxy.* His eyes turn to Rita and he smiles.

"We meet again," he says.

She takes his hand to shake it. "It's wonderful to see you again, Lord Morlin."

"You brought me back my sword." Morlin reaches behind his back and unlatches two sheaths from his belt. "And now I have brought one for both of you." He hands Rita the smaller one. It looks light yet powerful, radiating with energy in a dim purple glow. Rita pulls it from the sheath and swings it through the air. It zings with electricity and I step back. Morlin laughs and then gestures for me to take the other sword.

I reach for it, then stop.

"This sword is not like the dark sword, Bryn. It won't entice you to kill. It won't cloud your judgment."

I nod and attach the sheath to my belt.

"Now, we're ready to restore peace to the Galaxy," Morlin says.

Dad smiles at him and Rita lowers her sword. The air crackles with energy around the four of us, all with Gift powers, together in one spot. My skin breaks out in goosebumps. Each of our energies is different, and yet they seem to balance one another. Different strengths, but the same Gift.

A crack of lightning splits the sky on the horizon.

"We're ready now," Dad says. "It's time for us to finish this, together."

DEBRIEFING

RITA'S CURLS STICK OUT in every direction. Her untamed hair, when it isn't pinned back, will always remind me of how we made love for the first time, on Aylvon.

I hear my name and quickly turn my attention back to the meeting. Dad's at the head of the round table in the small meeting room. The Opposition Starship is large but very basic, compared to the Ruling Order Starships I'm used to. There's no holographic projector and the table isn't touchscreen.

I look around at the commanders. They seem competent enough, but will they still be alive after this is all over? Everyone from the Base is on board the ship and the families have been sent home.

"The crystal beam should reach Antineon in a few days," Dad says. "Fortunately it can't travel at quantum speeds." He looks at me and nods. "We had advance warning to be on the lookout for it."

Parrin sits silently a few seats down from Rita and me. He doesn't interrupt with any questions today, and has been uncharacteristically quiet since he spotted the ring on Rita's finger. Dad noticed it too, before the meeting started, and congratulated us. "We'll have a little celebration after the battle," he whispered as the others got settled into their seats.

Beeps' head turns left and right, swaying her body off balance as she sits on my knees. I get a better hold of her so she doesn't fall. There weren't any extra chairs in the small conference room and she wanted to be closer to me and Rita. Rita sets a hand on Beeps as she listens to Dad's debriefing. The ring on her finger glistens under the bright lights.

"We're working on a way to deflect the crystal beam before it reaches Antineon," Dad continues. "The wildlife both in and out of the water are still at risk." He brings up a star chart on a view screen behind him. "We've confirmed Dukath's vessel to be currently in the Sarbe Sector of the Quintiline star system. Rita, Bryn, and myself will confront him on his ship with a small team of Opposition fighters, while the fleet carries out a fabricated attack on the Ruling Order fleet. We need to make it appear like a sincere attack, while still keeping our flight crews safe. We don't need to do a lot of damage, just make them believe we are trying."

"Then why even attack?" one of the commanders asks.

"To make Dukath think he's winning." Dad glances at me. "The three of us will coerce Dukath into going to Antineon, for the black sword, where Morlin will be waiting for him."

I frown. How will we coerce Dukath? He's not easily tricked. He's usually the one doing all the manipulating.

Dad continues, not going into any further detail about how the three of us will convince Dukath to come to the catacombs on Antineon. Maybe he'll share the details with us privately, after the debriefing.

I glance at Rita. Her eyes looked glazed over as she watches Dad point out the fake attack strategy to the commanders.

I set my hand over hers. *What are you thinking about?*

She continues to look forward, grinning now.

The look on your face when I woke you up this morning with nothing on.

My cheeks heat up. I shouldn't have asked. The whole point of not searching her mind was so I wouldn't see anything that would get me too distracted during the meeting. But now my mind is filled with the thoughts of the way I woke up to this morning; Rita's kissing me and the heat of her skin against mine. I shake my head to dispel the tempting images. Fortunately Dad is already dismissing everyone and the meeting is over. The room fills with the sound of the chairs scraping the floors.

"Come on, Beeps," I say, setting her down to the ground. "Time to go."

Parrin is the first one out the door. Rita doesn't seem to notice and I'm glad, even though I do feel a bit sorry for the guy. He lost and he was the better man.

"Can I show you my new star system database?" Beeps says. "I got my old one updated. I can project one thousand new star systems! Including the Sarbe Sector where Dukath's starship is."

Rita leans down to her. "Sure," she says. "But first, Bryn and I are meeting with the General."

"But you just had a meeting now."

"Yes, but this one's even more important."

Beeps' head drops.

"After the meeting, we'll look at the stars in your new database, okay Beeps?" Rita says.

"Okay." She rolls back and forth slowly. "Parrin says when two people get married they stop being friends with everybody else."

"What?" Rita glances up at me then back at Beeps. "That's not true at all. How about we meet at my quarters after this session with the General and you can project some of your new star systems for us really soon?"

"Okay! Can Parrin come too?"

Rita hesitates for a second. "Yes, of course he can. If he wants to."

"I'll go ask him!" Beeps speeds away, moving easily on the carpeted floor. Rita straightens and crosses her arms.

"I have a feeling you might not like your dad's plan for taking down Dukath," she says, not looking at me.

"Why?" I ask.

"I talked to him about it back at the base. Our best chance is to let Dukath take me hostage so you can bargain for my freedom, in exchange for information on the whereabouts of the black sword. To make it seem legitimate."

"You're right." I push my chair in hard and it hits the table with a loud bang. "I don't like that plan at all."

Love and War

"**N**o," I say for the third time. Rita gives me an angry glare. She doesn't agree. We came to the mess hall to get a snack. Rita was already in her night clothes, which are far too tempting even when I'm upset. But our friendly late-night snack turned into a fight.

I cross my arms, refusing to back down from my position. There's no way we're going through with this crazy plan for trapping Dukath, it's just too dangerous to have Rita that close to him.

The hum of the propulsion engines vibrates throughout the ship as it makes its way to the Quintiline star system. We should reach our destination by wake hours.

"It's a good plan," Rita says, taking her warm drink to the nearest table.

I pretend not to hear her as I go get a drink. We've been arguing about this since the meeting with my dad and I refuse to argue anymore.

When I reach the food synthesizer I punch in the code for hot tea and wait. The mess hall lays in shadows; only the dim, off-hours lighting is on, glowing around the perimeter of the carpet. It's peaceful, with the humming of the ship and no one else here. Except that our fight anything but peaceful.

"Any plan that puts you in danger is not a good plan," I say, even though I had just decided to drop the subject and enjoy my time with Rita. She's obviously in no mood to listen to reason right now, so I don't know why I'm insisting.

"We're *all* in danger on this mission, Bryn," she says, taking a seat. "How else will we tell Dukath about the black sword and get him to go for it?" She waves her hand in the air. "Excuse me, Dukath, we just thought you should know the black sword is in the catacombs. You can go ahead and get it now." She frowns. "He'll know it's a trap. We have to make it look like he's bargained with my life for it."

I take a seat and grip my mug tight. "We'll just have to find another way."

Rita frowns down at her mug and doesn't take a drink. Great, I've started up the fight again.

"Bryn…" She says after a moment, her tone softer. "I know you're worried." She reaches up to touch my face and I pull away. I immediately regret it when I see the hurt expression on her face.

"Can we think about it?" I say, reaching for her to pull her into a hug. "And reconsider in the morning?"

She nods, but her body goes stiff and I stop trying to hug her.

"Why do you want to do this?" I ask, letting my arms fall to my sides.

She shakes her head. "I just want this to be over. As long as Dukath is still out there..." she stops. Is she still worried he'll take me away? I touch her arm and her shoulders relax slightly.

"Did you want something to eat?" I ask her, feeling like a jerk for arguing with her. She only wants to do what's best. But I can't stand the thought of Dukath being anywhere near her.

"I'm not really hungry anymore," she says softly.

"Chocolate?"

Thanks to Beeps, I now know that Rita loves chocolate.

She shakes her head and her eyes look sad.

I sigh. It's my dad I should be having this argument with, not Rita.

She leans forward and wraps her arms around my waist. I rest my chin on her head and eagerly return the hug. I don't want her to come on this mission at all, but she said there was no way she wasn't coming.

I rub her back gently.

The purple, nighttime lighting in the mess hall makes me think of our new swords.

"Do you think there's a fighting practice room on board?" I ask.

Rita pulls back and grins. "It's a Capital Starship, so there must be some training rooms." Her smile grows.

"I won't let you win this time," I tease.

"You won't have to."

"I accept that challenge." My fingers find their way into her hair and she closes her eyes at my touch.

"Don't try and distract me," she sighs.

I lean down to brush my lips over hers and she pulls away.

"Is that how you plan to win?" she jokes, her voice husky now. "Because it's not going to work."

"Are you sure?" I grab her arm just as she tries to run off. She squeals and tries to get free of my grasp but I don't let go.

"Not fair, you're taller," she says. "Let me go."

I get up to pull her against me but she traps me in a Gift hold and my throat tightens. I quickly let her go.

"You're stronger than I remember," I say. "But I know how to disarm you now."

I look down the front of her sleeping gown then send my thoughts to hers. She gasps in pretend shock, then releases me from her hold.

I scoop her up into my arms and her legs wrap around my waist. She kisses my cheek and my muscles go weak. I hurry to set her down onto the nearest tabletop.

"Are you trying to disarm me?" I ask. She's about to answer but I kiss her before she can reply. She returns the kiss and her intensity catches me off guard.

"Rita stop..." I break away, breathing hard. "Let's go back to my quarters first."

The lights flicker and the ship drops out of Quantum Drive, so abruptly that I stumble backwards and Rita falls off the counter.

I try to catch her but I hit the floor with a thump, Rita landing on me.

"Are you okay?" I say.

The hum of the ship's engine starts up again and it jumps back into Quantum Drive, making us both roll to the left.

"I'm fine," Rita says, getting up. "Did we do that?"

"Maybe," I say, trying to regain control of my fast-beating heart. "I think I may have let out some uncontrolled Gift energy after that kiss."

"Me too," Rita says, also a bit out of breath. "How about we save this for after the war?"

"Good idea."

"Rita!" Beeps comes rolling into the mess hall and Rita quickly adjusts the front of her night gown. "You didn't come see me so I could show you the star charts."

"Oh! Beeps!" Rita rushes over to her. "I'm so sorry. Bryn and I were just... getting a snack first."

"Will we still have time to look at the stars now?" Beeps asks. "It's past sleep time."

"We have all night," Rita says, putting her arms around Beeps.

"Did you forget about me because you're married now?" the little robot says.

I frown. Her socialization software didn't need any of Parrin's obvious influence.

Rita looks at me as though she's not sure what to say.

"No," I respond for her. "We'd wouldn't forget about you, Beeps."

Beeps turns her head in my direction then rolls away from Rita's arms to come over to me.

"I can show you the stars of Aylvon," she says. "Just like if you were there."

I smile. "I'd enjoy that."

Beeps replies with her happy sounds and rolls off, leading the way. Rita and I get up and follow her out of the mess hall. I take Rita's hand in mine and we exchange a glance. She doesn't seem mad at me anymore and I'm just glad we're not fighting. And that she's safe. For now.

* * *

"I'd like to go with you," Parrin says to Dad, the next morning. He steps in front of the elevator doors, stopping us from getting in. We're headed to the launch bay and now Parrin has appeared, insisting he join us. The Opposition pilots have already been dispatched to prepare for the faux attack and there's no time to waste.

Rita is with us, in her new uniform, all black, with dark gray stripes down the arms and the side of the legs.

Dad is in his General's uniform again, ready to face Dukath, under the pretense of a negotiations talk. The staged attack by the fighter jets is in theory a retaliation to Randon's crystal weapon threat on Antineon.

"You're not on the Primary Team for this mission," I say to Parrin. I push the elevator button and the doors open again.

"General," Parrin says to Dad, ignoring. "I'm well trained as a Ruling Order soldier."

I'm about to object but then decide to let Dad deal with it. The elevator doors close again.

"I know the layout of the Ruling Order ships," Parrin continues.

"As does Bryn." Dad says.

He puts a hand on Parrin's shoulder. "But I appreciate your enthusiasm to help."

I'm in awe of his patience with people like Parrin. I would have just put him to sleep or something, to shut him up.

"General, with all due respect," Parrin persists, "I'd like to be present at these negotiations, to protect Rita. In case Dukath gets into Takano's head again."

I grab Parrin in a choke hold so fast I don't recall deciding to do it.

"You're the one getting into everyone's head," I growl. "Your distrust of other team members' abilities. That's why you're not on the Primary Team."

"Bryn…" Rita touches my arm and I let Parrin go. He rubs his neck and looks at me like he wants to kill me.

"Parrin," Dad says. "You're not coming with us. It's already been decided. We need all the pilots we can get, especially one with your shooting expertise, to be in the attack against their ship."

He's being way too nice.

Parrin clenches his jaw, his face turning red. He turns sharply and marches off.

Dad and Rita both let out a sigh of relief once he's gone.

"You're right, Bryn," Dad says, pushing the elevator button, again. "We don't need any negative thinkers on this mission. Dukath will exploit any weaknesses he can, especially doubt."

The elevator doors slide open once more, and I wait for Dad and Rita to step in before I do. We head down to the launch bay in silence. I know Dad is right about Parrin, but I can't seem to shrug off his words, which have already planted a seed of doubt inside my mind.

What if Dukath does get the better of us somehow? He always seems to be one step ahead and knows how to exploit someone's deepest insecurities.

I rub my face with my hands. I have to stop thinking about it.

"Are you okay?" Rita whispers to me.

I nod. "I just want this to be over." I clench my fists, wishing we could simply obliterate Dukath with one blast of our combined Gift powers. But it's not that simple. He can't die, or I will.

But he can be locked away, for eternity. And then I can live on. It's what Rita wants. It's what we all want.

My stomach drops as the elevator comes to a stop.

It's time to face Dukath, and hopefully this time will be the last.

THE AWAY-TEAM (PART ONE)

"**WELL DONE, TAKANO.**" DUKATH leans back in his throne looking down at us from its height. "I see you've brought your father, too. How generous of you."

I shift on my feet, clasping my hands behind my back so Dukath won't see them shake. He's playing games already, but this time he can't get into my head and he knows it. It's a small victory for me, that he can't force his thoughts into mine anymore but has to speak out loud to be heard.

I look at his shriveled figure, hunched over on his seat. How did I ever once follow him? Admire him? But I'm no longer that lost boy who believes he has no other destiny than the one Dukath laid out before him. Rita has shown me a different future. A good one.

The large throne room is decorated with the statues of the ancient Masters, each one that Dukath killed over the years in order to strengthen the black sword.

He seems relaxed, as though he was expecting us to come. His throne sits at the end of a narrow, metal bridge which runs across an open space. There are no railings and the steep drop off the bridge reaches all the way down to the ship's energy core.

I suddenly feel unprepared for all that could go wrong with this plan. Even one false step on the bridge between us and Dukath and we'd fall to our deaths. Many commanders had lost their lives trying to cross this bridge, to get to Dukath.

I step in front of Rita and Dukath smiles.

"You won't win this time," I say to him, pulling out my sword. It feels light and less powerful than the black sword, which I'd become so used to.

"Won't I?" Dukath's grin widens and his confidence makes me want to slash him to pieces.

"We're here to negotiate," Dad says, his tone diplomatic. Dukath ignores him, turning his gaze to Rita.

"Takano Rynn has betrayed you before," he says to her. "And he'll do it again. Today."

"You're a liar," I yell. "Everything that comes out of your mouth is a lie." I point my sword at him. "Today, you will speak your last words."

Dukath wrings his gnarled fingers together, as though considering my words.

"We'll see." He grins.

The plan is to get him angry and then Rita will pretend to turn to his side, as though he's won her over with his powers of persuasion. Then, we will bargain for her release with giving Dukath the information about the black sword's location, as though we didn't want him to know it.

But I never actually promised to follow through with our plan.

"We'll tell you where the black sword is," I say to Dukath.

Dad and Rita gasp. I can feel their glares on my back. I've jumped ahead and put our plan out of order. My stomach clenches. This will still work. I have a plan of my own. Their shocked response helps it seem legit.

"If you stop the crystal beam, headed for Antineon," I continue. "I'll tell you where the sword is."

Dukath seems to think about this. "You would give me the black sword, just to save some crumbling ruins?" he asks.

Footsteps approach behind us.

"Supreme Leader."

I look over my shoulder and see Randon, once my friend, long ago. But there is no trace of that friendship left between us; Dukath saw to destroying it throughout the years.

So, Randon is alive. There were rumors, but no one knew for sure.

Randon ignores me and steps in front of us, before Dukath. His Ruling Order soldiers stand at attention near the front entrance.

"An Opposition fleet is preparing for an attack," he says.

Dukath waves his hand at him. "Let them attack."

"But Your Leadership—"

"Forget Antineon. Aim the crystal weapon at the fleet and disable their ships so they can't fly away. Then destroy them all."

"No!" Rita cries out. The sound pierces my soul and I shudder. Parrin is piloting one of the planes in the fleet. They were told to use evasive maneuvers and not take any real risks, but with the crystal weapon turned on them, their planes will stop working and they'll have no chance of survival.

I put my sword away.

Once again, Dukath has got the better of us.

THE AWAY-TEAM (PART TWO)

"**W**AIT!" DAD STEPS FORWARD. "Bryn is telling the truth. We're willing to give you the location of the sword, in exchange for the crystal weapon."

Dukath laughs out loud, the sound making my skin crawl. His laugh turns into a cough which seems so human and unexpected, for a man capable of such evil.

"Go," he commands Randon, once he's cleared his throat. "Kill them all."

"No!" Rita says. "I'll join you."

A silence falls over the room. I look at Rita. She's still trying to carry out our original plan of pretending to join Dukath. It's exactly what I was trying to avoid.

"Belay that order," Dukath says to Randon. "For now." He smiles.

"But, Your Leadership—"

"Disable the ships, but don't destroy them, yet."

Randon opens his mouth to say something more, but then shuts it again.

"Go on, then." Dukath waves is hand, but his gaze stays locked on Rita. There is a moment of silence, then Randon nods and walks out, his soldiers following after him.

"You'll join me, will you?" Dukath watches Rita, and I put my hand out in front of her.

"We'll give you the black sword," I say. "The all-powerful sword. It's got Rita's power in it too now, from the sacrifice of those she killed." I don't look at Rita, afraid of the pain I might see on her face at what I've said. "It's what you want, isn't it?"

"Perhaps." Dukath curls his fingers. "But perhaps I want more. Come forward, girl."

Rita doesn't move.

Dukath tilts his chin down and glares at her, his smile now gone. "I will have you, in exchange for the safety of the fleet. Is that not a fair agreement?"

Rita doesn't respond but holds Dukath's gaze.

"The young soldier," Dukath continues. "Who left the Ruling Order, to be with you. Parrin, is it? He's one of the pilots in the Opposition fleet now, is he not? Out there, flying around us right now."

"He didn't leave the Ruling Order to be with her," I say, unable to help myself.

I see the flicker of amusement in Dukath's eyes.

I'm letting him get under my skin.

"He was destined for her, Rynn. Not you."

Dukath keeps his eyes Rita. "Destined to give her children. Twin boys, if I'm not mistaken."

Rita gasps. "But I thought…"

"That's not true," I yell at Dukath.

"Quiet." He locks me in a choke hold and Dad raises his hand to stop him. But Dad's Gift is still unusable, unless Morlin lifted the spell with the incantation to free him to use his powers, and they haven't told me yet. I can't turn my head to look at him. I reach out with my thoughts instead.

I'm fine, I tell him, not wanting him to get in the middle of this.

He lowers his hand.

"Now, as I was saying." Dukath turns his attention back to Rita. "Let me give you some fatherly advice, seeing that your own father is not around to give it to you."

Don't listen to him, Rita, I try to say to her thoughts, but I can't tell if she can hear me.

"Takano Rynn will soil your destiny, your heritage as a princess. You've already broken the Gifted Masters' Ancient Code of Conduct, with this senseless attachment to him, and it will bring only pain and suffering upon you both."

Rita raises her hand toward Dukath and his hold on me eases slightly.

He smiles. "You're strong, child. Join me, and I'll let your pilot friend live. Then maybe there can still be a chance for you two, and for your future children. He can join with us, too."

"Never," Rita says in a low voice.

"As you wish." Dukath waves his hand in front of him. "I'll have the fleet destroyed."

"Wait."

"He's lying," I say to Rita, only now realizing that Dukath and Randon can't stop the direction of the weapon's crystal beam, now that it is set for Antineon. It can't be redirected that fast. "He's confusing you. There's no point in talking with him." I recall Charlie's report at the briefing. His team discovered that the weapon doesn't have enough synthetic crystals to recharge quickly for a new attack. It would take days.

I step up to the bridge walkway, my sword clutched in my hand. Heat from the warp core below wafts up, making me shiver in a feverish sweat.

"The crystal weapon can't be aimed at the fleet. It's already been launched for Antineon and there aren't enough synthesized crystals to aim on a new target," I say.

What else is Dukath lying about? Could he be lying about me dying if he dies? What if I wouldn't die? Is it a risk I'm willing to take? If I could know for sure, that our deaths weren't connected, I'd kill him instantly, right here and now.

"You will all drown in the oceans of Antineon, this very day," Dukath says, his voice rising. His hands grip the sides of his throne so hard they tremble.

I've irritated him. Good.

"I've just now foreseen it," he continues. "A senseless death, really. Unnecessary, when you could just join with me now and avoid such a tragic end."

"You're wrong," I say.

"My premonitions are never wrong. Your brother Morlin is about to be buried in the catacombs of the Temple on Antineon, at this very moment, the same place you are hoping to lure me. Am I right?"

Dad and I exchange a glance. Is Morlin in trouble?

Has Dukath known our plan all along?

He's mixing truth with lies, to confuse us, Dad says to me.

"My fleet is on its way now to destroy the Temple and sink it into the ocean."

"You can't destroy it," Rita says. "You'll bury the black sword too. It's there, in the catacombs."

Dukath doesn't reply but simply stares at her.

I want to get Rita out of here, I tell Dad. *Dukath won't go to Antineon. Not now. This plan isn't working.*

He answers, keeping his eyes on Dukath. *The crystal beam will reach Antineon in two days. After that, we won't be able to fly any ships on or off the planet, and then we'll never be able to bury Dukath there. We have to find a way to do this, now. This is our only chance.*

"Bring Randon," Dukath says to one of the soldiers still stationed at the door. "You want to save Morlin," he says to me, "and so you're lying about the black sword being in the catacombs. No matter. We will simply destroy Parrin's fighter plane."

"I'm not lying!" Rita yells. "The sword is there." She pushes her hand forward. "I'll show you!"

"Rita, no!" I cry out, but it's too late. Rita locks with Dukath's mind, opening a connection to him.

Rita, what are you doing?

"Yes." Dukath smiles. "I see it. The sword in a coffin. So, it is true."

I look to Dad. *We have to stop him.*

He nods and we focus our Gift energies forward.

Dukath glances at Dad. "Interesting," he mumbles, seeming unaffected by our efforts. "Your father has a bit of the Gift too, how nice."

Sweat drips down my back and suddenly it's becoming harder and harder to breathe.

"You've seen the sword and where it's been contained," Dukath says to Rita. "And it's under a spell which only Morlin can break. It seems that I do need him alive."

Break away from him, I try to communicate to Rita, but she's lost to me now.

I try to reach Dukath's mind, but it's impossible. Something is inhibiting my powers that I don't recognize.

"Supreme Leader," Randon says behind me again. "I've brought the crystal."

I want to turn around and kill him with my bare hands, but I can't move. He walks into my line of vision and I see that he's holding a large, blue crystal. I shut my eyes against its bright glow. My head begins to pound.

"Tell the pilots not to destroy the Antineon Temple yet," Dukath says to Randon. "There's something I want from there first. And we need Morlin alive as well."

"Yes, Your Supreme Leadership," Randon gives a curt bow then turns to one of the soldiers. "Find Parrin's Fighter plane and have it destroyed."

"Take Rynn and his father," Dukath says. "Have them stay in the special chambers prepared for them."

"Gladly." Randon walks past Dad with the blue crystal and he cringes in pain as it nears him. Then Randon approaches me, a satisfied smirk on his face. He holds the crystal up in front of me and I shut my eyes tight against the pain.

Why isn't it affecting Randon? It can't be the same crystal used with the weapon, which destroys all life forms.

It's only affecting Dad and I, draining our Gift energy. If Parrin were here, he'd be immune to its effects, like Randon is, because he's not Gifted. I should have let him come with us as back-up. He was right, and now we're going to die because I didn't listen.

"Meet your worst nightmare, Rynn." Randon pushes the crystal against my chest and I'm seized with a pain unlike any I've ever felt before. It shoots into my body, to my very bones.

"Randon..." I start to say, but have no energy to continue. He chooses not to remember, that we were once a team, even close friends at the Academy. He's finally getting his chance now to become the leader of the Ruling Order. I would have let him have it. I don't care about that anymore. But now I can't speak.

Dad cries out and the soldiers carry him away, the light of another dark blue crystal glowing in their hands.

Two other soldiers grab hold of me, and Rita moves suddenly, as though trying to come my aide.

"Not you, my child," Dukath says. "You, come forward."

Rita turns and steps onto the narrow bridge.

Rita, stop!

She can't hear me. She continues to walk onto the bridge.

"I see…" Dukath says to Rita. "How disgraceful, girl. You've already been with Rynn, haven't you? In a cave, on Aylvon."

A sick feeling settles into the pit of my stomach. But I can't make him stop talking.

"Your grandfather warned you to stay away from Takano Rynn. But you've ruined yourself now. And you killed many innocent Opposition soldiers, too. That is why your hair is cut short now, isn't it? Because you've turned your back on your Temple upbringing and used your Gift for evil. It has grown in power, through the death of the many you killed.

"And for what? All for a lifeless robot? Kra'an would be so disappointed in you, if he were still alive. He would strip you of your heritage and disown you. His prophecies also will now never come to pass, because of what you have done."

Rita's face crumples in an emotional torment that even I can feel.

Don't listen to him Rita, please.

Randon continues to hold the crystal close to my chest, and I can't reach Rita.

"You've mistaken your unnatural desires for love," Dukath says to Rita, seeming to enjoy her pained reaction. "And now you have done what is forbidden, an unlawful union with a Dark Master, a murderer, just like you, bringing shame upon your family name."

Rita's tears stream down her face, yet she is unable to wipe them away. My chest clenches.

"Come here," Dukath beckons her. "What a mess you've become, how dark and twisted, turning your sword against friends, because of some robot. And now this defiling of your body, with Takano Rynn. You've ruined everything that your parents wanted for you. They are still alive you know. I've found them. It's also where I found this crystal which will keep you captive, as it kept them captive all these years. I've decided to let them go. But they won't want you back now, not after you've destroyed everything you were destined to become."

Rita continues to walk forward on the bridge, still crying but unable to stop herself from moving forward.

Rita...

"Take them away," Dukath says to Randon, waving his hand in my direction. "Leave the girl to me."

Randon presses the crystal to my chest and everything goes black.

BReaKING OUT (PART ONE)

I WAKE IN A glowing blue, prison cell. The light makes it painful to open my eyes. The bars are lined with the blue crystal and so is the floor. I try to get up, but my body is too heavy.

"Dad?" I lift my head with effort and look around the cell. I see Dad in the cell beside me, unconscious.

"Dad!" I call again, louder this time. He doesn't respond and a panic grips me. I have to get him out of here. He's weaker than me, and a lot older. If I can hardly stand the effects of the crystal, it might actually kill him.

A loud bang against the bars startles me and I look over. A soldier appears down the hall, holding his gun in front of him. He joins the other one that is stationed at the end of the hall and they begin to talk quietly, then laugh.

Where's Rita? She wasn't brought to the holding cells with us. I close my eyes, not wanting to think about what Dukath's plans might be for her.

Mother, what do I do?

There is no reply.

My head falls back against the hard floor with a thud. Dukath was ready for us, with this crystal that can disarm our Gift powers. I shouldn't have let Rita come on this mission.

I close my eyes and see her in her night clothes, when we argued in the mess hall, just last night. I hate arguing with her. But maybe I should have argued harder. I should have stopped her, somehow, even if I had to put a sedative in her drink so she'd sleep for an entire day. Then she'd still be safe, back on the Opposition Starship right now.

I clench my fists, grasping for a last bit of hope which keeps wanting to slip away. What if Dukath was right, about Rita and Parrin's destiny? A cold chill moves through my body. No, he was just lying to hurt her and to discourage me. I can't let his lies get to me.

Or is it true?

If Parrin had a fair chance with Rita, and she hadn't come to my cave on Aylvon to find me in the first place, would they be together now? The thought is too much to bear.

The familiar sound of Beeps' wheels rolling over a smooth surface pulls me from my thoughts.

"Beeps?" I whisper, but my voice is drowned out by the vibrating hum of the cell bars.

I lift my head and see her roll up to the two soldiers at the end of the hall.

They look down at her.

"Is this one of our robots?" one of them asks.

The other shrugs.

Beeps rolls past them towards my cell.

"Hey!" the soldier yells. "Stop!" He raises his gun but before he can shoot, a phaser blast hits him from behind and he goes flying into the opposite wall. The other soldier turns to face the new threat, but he gets hit too, before he can shoot back. His armor takes the impact and knocks him unconscious.

Parrin appears, holding a large Ruling Order gun. He's breathing heavily, as though he's been running, and squints his eyes at the bright cell bars.

I never thought I'd be so glad to see Parrin in all my life.

He steps over the unconscious soldiers and hurries to our cell. When he finally sees me, he curses.

"You'd better be alive, Rynn," he mutters under his breath.

Breaking Out (Part Two)

"**Y**ou're heavy," Parrin grunts as he drags me across the blue floors. I want to tell him to hurry up, but don't have the energy. At any moment someone will realize what has happened and come barging in to stop us.

Parrin finally pulls me out of the blue cell and I roll onto my side.

"My dad..." I whisper.

"What?" Parrin asks, leaning in closer.

"Get the General."

He looks around then finally notices the other cell. "Oh!"

He hurries to open the cell doors, fumbling with the large set of keys. The crystal coating on the bars seem to have no effect on him.

I watch as he carries Dad under the arms, easily pulling him out of the cell. Dad's so much more fragile now than he used to be. It's humbling to see. He isn't moving. Parrin sets him down beside me.

I turn to Dad and reach for his hand.

"Dad?"

He has a faint pulse. Thank the stars. He's still alive.

The sound of Beeps' gears startle me. My strength is already returning, now that I'm no longer touching the blue floors. I motion to Beeps to join us. She rolls over.

"Where's Rita?" she asks.

I don't know," I say.

She lets out a high squeak.

"She was in the throne room, at the center of the ship, the last time we saw her."

"Can we go see if she's still there?" Beeps asks.

Parrin is already on his way out.

"Parrin!" I call after him.

Dad opens his eyes at my yell. Parrin stops at the end of the hall and looks back.

"We have to stick together," I tell him. "Wait for us."

He looks around the corner first, then walks back to us.

Dad sits up, holding his head in his hands. "What happened?" he says in a raspy voice.

"The blue crystal makes us weak," I say.

He looks to the cell doors, squinting at the glow. "Is Rita here?"

"No."

"We need to find her," Parrin says, sounding frustrated to be slowed down.

Dad looks at him. "Parrin? I thought you were flying a fighter plane on this mission."

"Sorry, sir. I know I disobeyed your direct orders." He glances at Beeps. "But it was Beeps' idea."

Dad shakes his head. "Well, then I'm glad you did." He starts to get up slowly and I get up to help. "Let's go find my daughter-in-law."

His words are like a small stab to my heart. I can't stop thinking about all that Dukath said, about Parrin and Rita.

I look over at Parrin. He's wearing that leather jacket again. His expression is serious.

If we find Rita, I'll let Parrin go to her first. He's the one who saved us on this mission. He deserves to be with her. She can think of him as the hero, and then decide if being married to me is what she really wants.

Parrin offers me his hand. "Can you walk?"

"Yes." I get up, not wanting his help. My legs are shaky but I feel stronger.

Parrin turns to Dad, when I don't take his hand, and helps him get to his feet.

"I'm fine," Dad insists.

"We need to hurry," Parrin says, picking up the large blaster he brought with him. "Follow me. I know a short-cut."

RESCUING RITA

W E HURRY DOWN A narrow passage. Pipes and electrical wires run along the low ceiling. I duck my head as I follow behind Parrin, who leads the way to the ship's core. My strength has returned and Dad seems a lot better too. We move fast. I can already feel the heat of the core reactor as we get closer to it. I wipe at my brow.

"Almost there," Parrin says over his shoulder.

I'm glad he knows the layout of the service areas beneath the corridors of the ship, since I never came down here when I was with the Ruling Order. This passage leads to the ship's energy core, below the throne room.

When we reach the end of the hall, I stop to catch my breath. I'm the only one who has to duck in the passage, Dad and Parrin are both short enough to keep standing.

I pull at the collar of my cloak which feels too heavy and is causing me to overheat.

Parrin reaches the reactor chamber first. The light from the core reactor bathes him in white. I squint to see past him. The core is massive and I wonder if our closeness to it will expose us to any dangerous radiation.

I follow Parrin into the reactor chamber and stand to my full height, tilting my head back. High above, I can see the metal bridge that connects Dukath's entranceway to his throne. I frown. It is quite far up. If Rita had fallen, she would be down here. The thought paralyses me.

I take a quick sweep of the room. I can't see the other side of the reactor but there's no sign of a body where we are. I have to believe Rita isn't dead. She could still be up there, with Dukath. It's impossible to hear anything over the loud hum of the ship's core reactor.

Parrin waves his hand at me to get my attention. He points to a metal ladder leading upwards. I nod and we run over to it.

The ladder extends up so high that I can't see the top of it. I start to climb and Parrin follows after me.

I jump from the ladder suddenly, off to the side so I don't hit Parrin on my way down. My boots land hard on the floor. Parrin gives me a questioning look.

I point up. "You go first," I say, although I don't think he can hear me. He nods and keeps climbing. Beeps bumps against my leg.

I scoop her up into my arms. "Can you hold onto me?" I ask her.

She nods and extends some clasps from her tiny doors, clipping onto the fabric of my shirt. I give her a smile. Parrin is already far up.

I start on my way up and Dad follows us. We climb in silence. My heart beats faster with each rung. Will Rita be up there? If not, where would Dukath have taken her? She has to be okay, she just has to be.

Parrin slows near the top, looking behind him toward the throne room entrance. The ladder is directly beneath the walkway, which blocks my view of the throne, and also keeps us hidden. Parrin presses his index finger to his lips, motioning for us to be quiet. I climb a little further up, then begin to hear voices.

"We tried, Your Supreme Leadership."

It's Randon.

"It's made of stone, is it not?" Dukath replies.

"Yes."

"Then open it!"

Beeps weighs heavy on me and I hold tight to the ladder, sweat dripping down back. We could wait until Randon and his guards leave and then try and take out Dukath with a surprise attack. But I can already feel the effects of the dark blue crystal energies, up at Dukath's throne.

"Don't make any noise," I whisper to Beeps.

"We tried everything," Randon continues. "The coffin is under some kind of spell."

"And what of Morlin?"

"He wasn't there."

"Enough!" Dukath yells, then begins to cough. "Must I do everything myself? How soon before the crystal beam reaches Antineon?"

"That's the problem."

There is no reply from Dukath. Randon seems to stumble on his next words. "It has already reached Antineon, therefore we can't fly ships into the atmosphere anymore and—"

"Stop your stammering Randon. I have a ship which can withstand the crystal weapon."

"But, sir, the beam is lethal to all life."

"It takes time to kill life forms, Randon. Am I a mere human? Full of weakness? I will not need to be there long, and I have a way out. The black sword is now made complete, with this girl's final, murderous act of violence. It is ready. Once I have it, everything will be set into place."

"Will you take the girl to Antineon, too?"

"If she goes to Antineon, she will die there. I have foreseen it."

I try to see around Parrin, but the walkway is directly above us, obscuring my view.

"Girl," Dukath snarls. "Tell me how I can get the black sword out of the tomb."

"I don't know." Rita's voice is hoarse and weak sounding, yet still defiant.

She's alive. But she sounds hurt.

"So, you're not willing to tell me. Shall I search your thoughts further?" Dukath says.

"Go ahead," Rita replies. "You won't find the answer. The tomb was sealed with the Gift and can only be opened using the Gift."

"And who is more gifted than I am? I will go and do it myself."

My palms become more and more sweaty, making it hard to hold onto the ladder. Rita is too quiet. She must be weak from the blue crystal which I can sense is up there. Why is Dukath keeping it in his throne room? Doesn't it affect him too?

I look down to see how Dad is doing. He's still holding on. We exchange glances but I can't communicate with him using the Gift. The crystal must be directly above us. I want to lean down to talk to him but Beeps is too much weight and I don't want to risk dropping her.

"Go!" Dukath commands in a loud voice. "Prepare my ship." His voice sounds from halfway down the walkway now, and I hear the shuffle of his steps.

"What about her?" Randon says.

"Keep her alive."

"Shall I take her to one of the crystal prison cells, Your Leadership?" Randon's footsteps move down the walkway as well.

"Keep her here and away from the others in the holding cells. I don't want her anywhere near Rynn. Post guards outside."

I catch a glimpse of Dukath's back as he walks towards the doors at the other end of the bridge.

He moves slowly, hunched over like an old man. He's nothing but a lonely, bitter old Master, who finds pleasure in the suffering of others.

But he's heading for Antineon, right where we want him. Our plan has been set into motion after all.

Dukath and Randon's steps retreat through the front entrance and the doors slide shut behind them. Then, there is only silence.

Parrin looks down at me from above. His forehead glistens with sweat. I nod for him to keep going up. He goes to the top of the ladder, then struggles to climb over the bottom part of the walkway. I reach my hand out to use my Gift energy and give him a boost, but it doesn't work. Parrin's hand slips and I try harder. Parrin catches his footing and finally makes it over the side.

"Rita!" Parrin's shocked cry startles me and I climb faster. My arms shake as I pull myself up over the ledge of the bridge. I set Beeps down with a loud clank. She unclasps from me and zooms ahead.

"Rita!" she beeps.

Parrin is on his knees, holding a limp Rita in his arms, in front of Dukath's throne. She's covered in shining blue metal straps, clasped around her body. Parrin struggles to remove them, his movements clumsy and desperate.

He looks over at me. "I can't get these things off of her!"

The crystal on Rita's restraints makes me nauseous, even from where I'm standing, at a distance. The familiar pain of the crystal's effects begins to settle into my bones again.

"Bryn!" Parrin yells. "Help me."

"I can't." I clench my fists.

"Bryn!" Dad calls up from below. I lean over the edge of the bridge and reach my arm down to him. He looks pale and weak.

"Dad, grab my hand."

My stomach tightens. I'd forgotten all about him. He could have slipped and fallen.

He grabs my hand and I pull him up with a grunt. We sit on the narrow bridge pathway, catching our breath.

"I can help," Beeps says to Parrin. She pulls out a small screwdriver and begins to unscrew the tiny hinges of one of the metal straps around Rita's wrists.

Dad puts a hand on my arm. "We need to move farther back," he says. "Away from the crystal."

He's right. It's making me lightheaded and the bridge is dangerously high up.

We get up with some effort and walk down the narrow bridge to the other side. I grip Dad's shoulder, glad that he's alive and made it this far.

Don't worry Bryn, he says. *It will all work out.*

I nod and we watch as Parrin and Beeps work together to remove each metal band around Rita's body. Parrin is clumsy, but determined. If he was meant to be with Rita, then I won't stand in his way anymore. I can't even help her right now. It's Parrin who's saving her, Parrin who would make a good future partner for her.

The green crystal from Rita's ring catches the light, glistening for a moment on her limp finger. I was selfish to give it to her. I wanted her all to myself, but I wasn't thinking of what was best for her.

Beeps continues to unlatch the metal bands. It's agonizing to watch her and Parrin's slow progress, knowing that the guards are stationed just outside the throne room doors and Randon could return at any moment to find us here, helpless and weak.

Parrin removes another band from around Rita's knee, then ankle, his movements gentle. Her head rests on his shoulder. She watches him work with a glazed-over look in her eyes. Her breathing seems too heavy and I can't even imagine the pain she must be feeling with all that crystal around her. Her head turns and she sees me at the other end of the bridge.

"Bryn?" she says softly. Her throat sounds dry.

Parrin and Beeps remove another band and then she's finally free. She crawls towards the bridge that's separating us.

"No, wait!" Parrin says. "There's one more."

She stops and tries to help him to remove the remaining band, then flinches when her fingers touch it.

"It's okay. I'll do it," Parrin tells her. "We're almost done." Beeps loosens another restraint on Rita's ankle and it clatters onto the floor. Parrin pushes the blue pieces towards the edge of the bridge and they fall down below. The moment all the crystal is gone Rita stumbles to her feet and I run to her across the bridge.

I fall onto my knees in front of her and throw my arms around her waist. I don't care that Parrin and Dad are watching.

She wraps her arms around my head and I bury my face in her chest. She lowers down onto her knees too and kisses me. My strength returns. Our love for each other makes our Gift stronger. It isn't anger and hate that give the Gift its full power, the way Dukath taught me.

I cup Rita's face in my hands. "Rita, I love you. I want to protect you, forever."

"We'll protect each other," she says, smiling through her tears.

I shake my head, swallowing down the lump in my throat. I wasn't able to protect her this time.

"If you were meant to be with Parrin, then—"

"What?" Rita shakes her head. "You're the only one I want to be with. I don't care what Dukath says. It's you I love" She hugs me and I close my eyes, savoring her warm embrace.

Beeps rolls over to us. "Are we done with the mission now?"

Rita lets me go and turns back to Beeps. "We're not done yet," she says. "But as soon as we are, we're going to play that constellations game you liked so much, okay?"

"With my new star chart holograms?"

"Yes."

"Okay!" Beeps spins in a circle and Parrin smiles. "Can Parrin play too?"

"Yes, of course." Rita walks over to Parrin and gives him a hug. "Thank you," she says to him. "For coming, even though we told you not to."

He blinks, then hugs her back, glancing over at me as though he's worried I'm going to get mad.

Dad joins me and sets his hand on my shoulder. Rita walks over to us and takes my hand. Parrin stands on the other side of Dad and we stand together.

"We're almost there," Dad says to us. "I may not be able to see into the future, but I see the faces before me, faces of the most powerfully Gifted in the Galaxy."

Parrin shifts his weight on his feet.

"That includes you too, Parrin," Dad continues. "You're as brave as any Gifted person I've known, and you'll join us on this final mission. We're going to take down Dukath once and for all."

DOUBT

"**W**E CAN'T GO THROUGH the doors," Parrin says, stating the obvious. "Should we climb back down the ladder?"

"Yes. We have to hurry." Dad goes to the edge of the bridge, making me tense with worry.

"I'll help lower you down," I say to him.

Now that the crystal chains Dukath had on Rita are gone, I should be strong enough to help Dad and Rita. I glance back see make sure she's okay. She seems to have regained her strength and looks beautiful, like a ray of sunlight amidst the dark walls and bleak statues in the throne room.

"I can get us back to our ship through a sanitation chute," Parrin says. "If our ship is still in the same place we docked it."

"What if Randon discovers we're gone?" Rita says, joining us at the ladder.

"They've gone to Anineon for the sword," Parrin says.

"Randon won't go," I say. "He'll stay here."

I steady Dad as he gets onto the latter, then he starts to climb down. I take a step back, away from the ledge. My vision spins for a second and I rub my eyes. This is the worst time to suddenly be hit with a fear of heights.

"You okay, Rynn?" Parrin says.

"I'm fine." I hold my hand out to Rita. "I'll help lower you down next."

She takes my hand. Her grip is strong, stronger than Dad's was. I give her a smile. She'll be okay.

I'm the last to go down and I try to ignore my shaking hands and dizziness. I glance up, half expecting to see Randon leaning to look over the side of the bridge, pointing a blaster down at me.

Once I reach the bottom, my balance returns and my vision clears, despite the fact that we're now closer to the blue crystals, which landed down here somewhere.

Parrin, Dad and Rita are already at the entrance of the maintenance tunnel. They seem to be arguing.

"I heard what Dukath said!" Parrin yells at Rita as I approach. "He said if you go to Antineon, you'll die."

Rita crosses her arms. The look in her eyes makes even me nervous, and I'm not the one arguing with her.

"I heard him too," she says to Parrin. "But I'm choosing not to listen."

"Maybe you *should* listen," Parrin argues.

"You're telling me to listen to Dukath?" Rita yells, over the hum of the core reactor. I tense, wondering if their fight will draw attention to our escape.

"I'm telling you to stay alive!" Parrin looks to me for back-up, but I don't offer any.

"We're stronger together," Dad says. "That's how we got away from the holding cells and that's how we'll defeat Dukath."

"The crystal beam is lethal," Parrin says.

"The ships can't fly there," Beeps says.

A look of concern passes between us as we all seem to realize she's right.

"Then it's settled, we're not going." Parrin turns to walk away.

I hesitate, wondering if I should tell everyone that Dukath has two ships, fit to withstand the effects of the crystal weapon. He likely took the larger one. The smaller craft is for emergencies and can hold all four of us. I remember using it on one a trip to a planet with high radiation. But what if Parrin is right and we should keep Rita away from Antineon? We could just escape and run from Dukath. Maybe if we go far enough, he won't find us. He'll have the sword he wants so much. He might not care about us anymore.

I glance around at the frowning faces of the others.

Rita won't want to run. She won't want to leave the Galaxy in jeopardy, just so we can get away and be safe.

"There are two."

"What?" Rita says.

"Dukath has two ships that can withstand the radiation. I can try to get us the second one."

"Great!" Rita squeezes my arm. "Come on then, we need to go." She ducks under the short door frame that leads into the passageway beyond. I follow after her, wanting to keep Parrin away from her in case he starts another fight.

I stop at a control panel. Would Randon have reset the access codes since I was last on this ship? I punch in the numbers used by Commanding Officers, but not my own code. I don't want to take the chance that it would alert the system.

"Bryn, hurry up," Parrin slams into me from behind.

"Just a moment."

The maintenance system home screen pops up.

Good. The Commanders' codes still work. Now I can get us into the docking bay at least. Then we'll find that ship. I can use my Gift influence to trick the guards. Even Randon discovers us, we'll be gone before he realizes what's happened. Hopefully.

I leave the control panel and we hurry down the hall.

Dukath is on his way to Antineon, right where we want him, and now we have the element of surprise. He won't be expecting us. This just might work.

THE BATTLE OF ANTINEON

THE ISLAND LOOKS DESERTED when we land. I reach for my sword, a habit from years of relying on it. The replacement sword that Morlin gave me feels inadequate compared to the black sword. But it's not going to be a sword that will defeat Dukath in the end.

No one says anything as we remove our harnesses and get up from our seats.

There isn't really a plan here, only one goal; destroy Dukath. And if we don't do it fast enough, we might all die in the attempt. Parrin will be the first to die from the radiation if we stay here too long, being the weakest.

If I didn't know him better, I'd admire his bravery. He's the first one through the hatch doors.

Dukath's words haunt me. *He was destined for her, Rynn. Not you. To give her children, twin boys.*

I shake my head. The future isn't written yet, even the prophecies need a specific course of events to make them come to pass. And yet, Dukath's comment about Rita still makes me uneasy. *If she goes to Antineon, she will die there.* He was speaking to Randon and there was no reason for him to be lying to Randon about what he foresaw.

I take Rita's hand before she can jump out of the ship.

"Let's do this together, okay?" I say to her. I don't add the rest of what I'm thinking, that if she dies, I will not want to live without her. She leans in and gives me a quick kiss on the lips.

"We'll end this, today," she says.

I nod and squeeze her hand, then we jump out into the fog together.

* * *

"He's not down here," Parrin calls up from the catacombs below.

The wind blows cold and relentless through the cracks in the old temple walls, howling like angry spirits. There's no sign of Dukath. But we couldn't have beat him here, he left before us. Could he already have the sword and be gone?

I shake my head. The effects of the radiation are already making me disoriented.

Rita crouches near the entrance, her expression unreadable.

"Are you sure?" Dad calls down to Parrin.

"I sense him," Rita says. She looks up at me and I see fear in her eyes.

I grip my sword tight. If she can sense Dukath then does that mean he can sense her as well? Does he know we're here? Will he manipulate her again? After what she just went through, it is no wonder she looks afraid. I want to tell her to go back to the ship and fly as far away from here as she can, but I know she won't listen.

She gets up and turns abruptly, pulling out her sword.

"Rita?" I reach out to her but my hand misses, like I'm not able to tell distance in the fog. I shake my head. Isn't the radiation also affecting Rita?

She runs off into the fog.

"Rita! Wait!"

I turn to Dad. He wipes his arm across his eyes and blinks.

"He's here. Rita's gone after him."

"Dukath—?"

"No, Morlin," Dad says.

Parrin appears at the opening in the ground and climbs up from the ladder below.

Rita's already at the stone stairs that lead up above the fog and into the sunset.

"Parrin," I point my sword at him. "Come with me."

I don't wait for his reply but run after Rita. When I get to the stairs, I take them three at a time. The ocean rages below and the waves crash against the rock island. The water splashes the stone steps, making them slippery.

Rita... wait. Be careful, I call out to her.

She reaches the top before I do, and a flash of lightning blinds me for a moment, making me lose sight of her. I sway and my foot steps off the edge.

A hand grabs my arm and pulls me back.

"Careful, Bryn," Parrin says.

I steady myself then start walking again. "We need to get to Rita. She can't go off alone. We have to stick together."

Suddenly screams from somewhere in the fog. I can't tell from which direction. The wind howls, blowing debris against my face.

"Rita!" I hurry up the last of the steps and climb onto a stone platform, the highest lookout point of the old Temple.

Dark clouds gather wildly in the sky above and the air crackles with electricity. The beam from the crystal weapon is changing the weather, already poisoning the planet, and us, if we stay here much longer.

Another flash of lightning lights up the sky and I see Dukath, wielding the black sword and swinging it at Morlin.

They're in the middle of a battle, which Morlin is clearly losing. He falls to his knees, clutching his side in pain.

Dukath towers over him. He is no longer the hunched over, pitiable master we saw back at the throne room. His eyes now glow red and he's standing at his full height, his body larger and taller than before. He swings his sword down and Morlin rolls out of the way before it hits him.

I hurry to help him, but Rita is already there. Dukath laughs, his face is changed somehow, no longer the hollow face of an old man, but the image of one of the Masters I killed long ago. I freeze, watching as his face changes yet again, morphing into all the dead Masters I'd killed over the years to strengthen the black sword.

I step back, unable to look at all those I murdered. Their lives are in the sword now.

The wind swirls violently around us and I stumble to the side, the horizon tilting before me.

"Takano!" I hear Rita cry, but I'm too disoriented and dizzy to see where she is. The radiation is blocking my concentration. She cries out again and her urgency snaps me out of my daze.

I look up to see Dukath block an attack from Rita's sword. She's thrown back by the force of the black sword but slows her fall with her Gift. Our eyes meet.

We have to defeat Dukath. This is our chance.

Morlin gets up, returning to fight with what little strength he has left.

Rita runs to me and takes my hand.

"Let's jump together and attack," she says over the howling wind.

I nod and we run full speed, towards Dukath.

Morlin falls again and Dukath raises the black sword to finish him off.

Rita squeezes my hand and we jump at the same time. She lets my hand go and we both raise our swords above our heads. Dukath turns in surprise. With a loud cry I slash down just as Dukath swings to block my blow. But he doesn't stop Rita's sword. She hits his shoulder and he cries out.

A burst of energy from the black sword throws us both back and I land hard on my shoulder. My vision blurs.

"Bryn! Watch out!" Rita cries. My eyes clear just as the black sword comes down at me.

I roll away but Dukath freezes, his attention now elsewhere. I turn to see where he's looking.

Morlin is standing in front of Dad, one arm outstretched towards him. His voice travels on the wind, the words foreign, ancient; the incantation to return Dad's full use of his Gift.

A cloud of energy swirls around Dad. I can feel its power, as though the years of not using his Gift strength have built up and now he is releasing it all at once. Morlin drops to the ground and Dad turns to face Dukath. The anger in Dukath's eyes wavers for a second and is replaced with a look of uncertainty.

"Dad!" I yell. His physical body isn't strong enough to hold all that power.

I reach out to him and Rita joins me.

Dukath snarls at us but he can't move now. His red eyes look from Rita, to me, then Dad. A moment of doubt crosses his face. He underestimated our united strength.

I see Parrin run to Morlin, whose blood now flows from his side, darkening the stone floor beneath him.

The cry of the eagle above us pierces through the rushing sounds of wind and waves. I take Rita's hand, the effects of the crystal beam clearing a bit with the simple touch between us. Thunder rumbles, shaking the stone ground and the entire temple on the small cliff island. It could crumble into the ocean at any moment.

The low ceiling of dark clouds moves and swirls above Dukath's head.

"You will die today," his voice booms, his eyes on Rita. He fights against our hold and I feel my strength wavering, but Rita remains strong. She's more powerful than I am. Is this why Dukath wanted her alive, to fight on his side? Because she is so strong?

Despite the hundreds who died to strengthen the black sword, just the few of us using our Gifts together at the same time, are still stronger than all the dead. We've stopped Dukath momentarily, but my strength is fading fast and so is Dad's.

The wind picks up speed, whipping dust and debris all around. I'm pushed back suddenly by an unseen force. I fight against it, stepping forward again.

Dukath's strength is returning.

One of us has lost our hold on him.

"Bryn!" Dad calls out.

I can't turn to him, or reply. I need all my focus to be on Dukath, otherwise he'll break free.

"The waves are getting too high," I hear Dad yell.

Energy builds in the air, sizzling on my skin. The blades of our swords seem to be reacting with the crystal that is now in the planet's atmosphere. My strength is weakening, but so is Dukath's.

I close my eyes and think of Master Kra'an's words, which he spoke to me when I was little.

A mountain or a grain of sand are both moved with equally effort, in the Gift. No more or less strength is needed for either, only a more focused concentration.

I call out to the energy around me, in so many different forms. It isn't just Rita, Morlin and I who have strength to fight Dukath. I can pull strength from it all: The clouds and lightning, the wind, the sky, even the beam of crystal energy breaking through the outer layers of Antineon's atmosphere. I draw their energies together into one spot.

A bolt of lightning illuminates the sky and a loud crack of thunder booms in my ears. The lightning shoots straight down at Dukath. His cry goes unheard in the rage of the storm around us. He drops the black sword and it tumbles across the rocks.

"Bryn!" Dad yells behind me.

I reach for the black sword just as a wave of water washes up onto the rock platform, knocking me off my feet. The water retreats back towards the ocean below, pulling the sword with it. It disappears over the edge of the cliff.

"Bryn!" Dad yells. He's been swept up in the wave as well and is being pulled to the cliffs edge.

"Dad!" I reach for him with my Gift, using what little strength I have left. The wind and rain beat against me, making it hard to focus. He's too far away to get a clear hold on.

I scramble to my feet and run to him, but he's pulled over.

I fall to my knees on the slippery stone and grab his hand just as he flies over the cliff side. My body slams against the hard stone, but I hold on tight. Dad shouts something but the storm rages too loudly for me to hear. The dark waters retreat, preparing for the next large wave to come.

"Hold on!" I yell.

I find a foothold in the rocks and pull Dad back up with a loud grunt. He tumbles forward.

Rita! he says to my thoughts. *Dukath threw her off the side of the cliff.*

The rain is now falling in sheets, blocking my view.

I turn in all directions, but don't see Rita.

"Rita!" I yell.

Dukath stands in the downpour like a monster, larger than life, his shoulders heaving as though he's laughing.

"Rita!" I call out again, trying to get a sense of where she could be.

"Bryn," Dad grabs my arm. "Over there!" He points towards the cliff's edge on the other side. "She went over on that side. Forget Dukath. It's not possible to defeat him. He's too strong now that we've lost Rita."

I run to the cliff's edge and a blast of energy from behind pushes me forward. It's Dukath. There is nothing in front of me to help me stop the forward motion and I'm thrown out over the ocean below. I turn in mid-air, looking for something to latch onto behind me with my Gift, but the cliff is too far away from me.

I look down at the dark waters below and my stomach drops at the all too familiar sight. This is how I almost died last time, only this time I want to live.

The cry of an eagle cuts through the storm and I catch a glimpse of the large bird. Its wings flap with effort as it carries Rita in its talons, slowing its descent, to set her limp body onto a flat rock out on the ocean.

I drop into the water with a sudden shock of cold. My chest grips tight in response, knocking the breath out of me, reminding me again of the last time I fell into the oceans of Antineon.

I kick off my boots and unlatch my heavy cloak as fast as I can. My fingers fumble with my belt, too cold to work properly.

I unclasp my sword at the last moment before my belt and cloak sink into the depths below.

My lungs burn as I fight to swim back up.

If she goes to Antineon, she will die there. Dukath's words invade my thoughts.

I won't let Rita die here. I won't lose her again.

A wave throws me into the cliffside and pain shoots through my shoulder.

The wave retreats and I grab onto the roots of a lonely tree growing in a crack of stone. I take a big gulp of air before the next wave hits and pushes me into the rock wall with another strike to my shoulder.

I pull myself up the tree's trunk and climb onto a narrow rock ledge.

Across the waters I see the massive bird sitting tall beside Rita, as though guarding her. Rita is lying on her side, unmoving.

Another wave crashes into me, almost knocking me off the rock ledge again. I get a better hold of the small tree and brace myself for the next wave. I won't be able to swim to Rita from here. I have a better chance of boosting myself with my Gift and jumping over to the rock she's on.

I look up. The top lookout point is no longer visible from where I am.

Dad! I cry out, but there's no response.

Dukath will try and kill him. He's still up there. So is Morlin. They could die.

I can't help them all.

They'll survive, I tell myself. They're strong. I can't lose hope now. I have to get to Rita. She's still on that rock, unconscious.

A large wave rises up and suddenly I don't see Rita anymore. I freeze, my body going cold. The next moment the wave retreats and I see she's still there, with the eagle beside her. Its dark eyes look right at me, as though waiting for me.

I take a big breath and leap out across the waters, pushing off the stone cliff behind me, my Gift boosting me forward.

The waves reach up for me, trying to grab at my feet as I fly through the air.

I hit the edge of the flat rock with a hard thump, knocking the breath out of me. I slide back toward the water.

My foot catches on a crack in the side of the rock and I stop myself from sliding off. I climb up quickly, before another wave comes to wash me away.

The great eagle sits patiently, watching me with calculating eyes. I can now see its labored breaths, its beak open as the majestic bird pants for air. The effects of the crystal beam are also wearing it down.

Thank you, I say, but the eagle makes no acknowledgement of my thanks.

I crawl over to Rita. She's freezing cold, her clothes soaked and her skin is pale. I pull her into my lap. Her arms fall limp and her head rolls to the side.

I touch her cold cheek, turning her face to me. Her lips are blue.

"Rita?" My heart races. I set my hand to her throat to check for a pulse.

There is none.

"No!" I take her wrist in my hand. Again there is no pulse. "Rita...?"

A stillness settles around me and the waves calm. The rain stops beating down and the wind withdraws, leaving a reverent silence in which the absence of Rita's beating heart is all too noticeable. The only sound is that of my heart pounding in my ears. It's as though time itself has stopped and can't exist without Rita.

Dukath was right.

And I knew he was. I knew and I should have stopped Rita from coming here. I should have tried harder to keep her safe.

The cold of Rita's body seeps into my arms and chest.

I look up, sensing someone's gaze on me. High at the top of the Temple stands Dukath, at the edge of the cliff. He's watching us and smiling.

My body trembles with an anger so fierce it burns through to my very core. I lower Rita down gently, my eyes still on Dukath.

I'm going to kill him.

And if I die too, then I don't care.

Free

I LEAP OFF THE rock's edge with an upward blast of energy, fueled by rage so strong that I fly straight to the high lookout point and land in front of Dukath. His smirk wavers for a second when he sees me. My eyes burn with anger. Then he smiles, as though my reaction to Rita's death is amusing to him.

"Tragic," he says. "But I warned you that she would die if she came here."

I reach forward and the black sword flies out of Dukath's hand into mine.

My focus sharpens as the sword's power fills me. It sparks with energy, reacting to my hatred for Dukath. His form is already crumpling back to the shriveled old man he was before, now that he no longer holds the black sword.

I don't hesitate but pierce him through, before he even knows what's happened. His eyes grow wide as though with disbelief.

"No…" he hisses. "You can't kill me…"

"I warned you too, Dukath," I say. "That you would die today."

Dukath drops onto his knees. "I can't be killed, you insolent, worthless fool, you can't kill me…" His words become garbled and his final cry cut off.

A gust of wind lifts his cloak, then it settles flat onto the rock surface, his form beneath it small and lifeless.

I drop the black sword and it spins on the rock surface, before becoming still.

So much power, so much death, all in one sword. I reach down and pick it up again.

I've defeated Dukath. But if he can't ever die, as he says, then I won't die because of him either.

I put the sword in my sheath, then wrap Dukath's large cloak around his limp body.

In the tombs below, he will be contained forever. Once the radiation has fully seeped into everything on this planet, he can never leave. The souls of the dead Masters will accompany him for all eternity.

I lift Dukath onto my shoulder and stand with effort, my strength faltering for a moment.

There is no sign of Parrin or Morlin, or Dad. But I need to take care of this. I need to know Rita didn't die in vain and that Dukath will never rise again.

I will finish this once and for all. For Rita.

For the entire Galaxy.

The crumbling steps are easier to manage going down, than up. I try not to think about Dukath's body on my shoulder. His blood drips down onto the stone and I realize I was never quite sure if he was human or not. Perhaps he isn't, and yet he bleeds.

I consider simply dropping him into the hole that leads down to the catacombs, then climbing down after to stow him in a stone coffin. But I can't do it. I can't throw his body down like a discarded piece of garbage. Even after everything he's done, he was my master. And he's come to a pitiable end.

I lower to my knees to find the ladder that leads down into the catacombs.

Dukath was a father to me, when my own father wasn't. And although he wanted nothing but to use me to help him become the greatest ruling power in the galaxy, he did believe in me. He believed I'd be part of that grand plan.

I climb down the ladder, using one hand, the black sword burning at my side.

Dukath had no capacity to care about me. He was evil and wanted me to be the same. He wanted to kill the part of me that was human, but he didn't succeed. Rita didn't let him.

The green fog in the catacombs is now an orange color, perhaps reacting to the crystal beam infiltrating the planet. I cough, the dust thick and hard to breathe in. The coffins lie silent on either side, bathed in orange. I hurry to the one which had the secret passage behind it, where we found Rita.

My knee gives out as I step over the coffin and I land hard on the dirt floor. Dust billows up around me and I cough again, holding my cloak up to my mouth to keep from breathing it in.

The black sword is hot against my side now, reacting with the crystal in the air.

I have to hurry. Parrin or Dad will not be able to get off this planet without help. Unless Dukath already killed them, too.

I drop to my knees in front of the coffin at the end of the narrow hall, then place Dukath's body into it. The lid is still off, since the last time we were in here. I pull the black sword from my belt. It glows red now and the heat of the handle burns my palm. I set it onto Dukath's cloak, which is still wrapped around him. It makes a sizzling sound and a burning smell wafts up.

My lungs are ablaze with the dust in the air and I quickly set the lid onto the coffin, my hands slippery with sweat. Stone grates on stone as I slide the lid shut. Dust blows out from all sides as it latches into place with a final loud clank.

The stone suddenly becomes scorching hot and I pull my hands away. The heat from the coffin is so strong that I can feel it on my face. I step back, watching as the lid and coffin melt together, sealing it shut.

Voices begin to shout, echoing from all directions, distant sounding, yet very present. I turn to leave, my strength returning, as though fueled by a power from the voices, encouraging me to hurry; to return to Rita out on the rock.

I don't look back to the coffin, which will now forever hold Dukath.

It's finally over.

But Rita is gone.

I climb back out of the cave and onto the faded marble floors of the sanctuary. The eagle cries out, somewhere above. It's the same cry I heard the last time I felt this much despair.

Rita...

I look up. Is Rita looking down at me through the eagle's eyes?

I run to the edge of the cliff where the ruins have crumbled and left the rest of the Temple open to the sky and ocean. My breathing comes easier, now that I am no longer down in the dust of the catacombs. I look for Rita. Her body is still there, on a large rock out on the ocean. The waters are now calm.

I must take her with us. I'm running out of time. I push off the side of the cliff, my a renewed sense of urgency giving me a final burst of strength. This time I jump far enough to make it onto the rock all in one leap. I land with a heavy slap against the flat surface, my feet still bare after losing my boots to the ocean.

Rita's curls lie over her face. I lift her into my arms and smooth her hair aside. Her skin is so white, it seems to glow.

The eagle circles above.

In the power of the Gift, we have life, not death. I hug Rita close and repeat the mantra Morlin taught me long ago.

With the Gift we bring peace and balance and life... Another voice joins with mine in my thoughts. It's Morlin. He's reaching out to me. He's still alive, on this island somewhere.

I stop to listen to his words.

As the Eagle flies
The body of Rita lies
Waiting for the return
Of her soul, from the skies

Morlin has foreseen this. Rita has a greater purpose than to simply die here on this planet.

The great eagle spreads its wings wide in flight, blocking out the sunset rays. I look up and see the bird tilt its head back with a strangled cry.

Rita suddenly gasps in my arms and water comes out of her mouth. She sits up quickly and turns onto her side, coughing up more water.

I hear a loud splash and turn to see that the massive bird has fallen out of the sky, into the waters below.

Thank you.

I close my eyes for a moment, then lower my face down to the stone.

"Bryn?" Rita says. She sets a cold hand onto the back of my head. "Bryn, are you okay?"

It's finally over. Rita and I are free.

THE SECReT

"STANDING IN FRONT OF a group of people to tell them we've decided to love each other forever..." Rita sighs against my chest. "It just seems so unnecessary. It's a decision we already made. It has nothing to do with them."

I run my hand over her back. The silky feel of her night clothes is not nearly as nice as the smoothness of her bare skin. I look out the window of Rita's quarters, at the stars outside. They're not rushing by, like they would be at Quantum Speed. There's no hurry now to get anywhere. We're on our way to Rita's home planet and there isn't anywhere else I'd rather be at the moment, than right here on this ship, with her in my arms.

Rita plays with the ring on her finger, her hand resting on my chest.

"It's not their decision if we get married or not," I tell her. "But it affects them too, so a public ceremony is appropriate."

"I suppose..." Rita starts to run little circles with her finger on my chest, as though thinking.

My heart beats harder and I hope she doesn't ask me too many questions. It's so hard to keep secrets from her. I've avoided speaking thoughts to her with the Gift for the past three days, so she won't find out what we're planning as a surprise for her. But it's getting harder and harder not to accidentally say something.

Parrin, Charlie and a small team of Opposition soldiers are out looking for the blue crystal planet, where we believe Rita's parents might be. Parrin and Beeps overheard Dukath talking about the dark blue crystal planet, while they were on his ship and looking for us. They believe Rita's parents were enslaved on it and might still be there.

Beeps found the coordinates from Dukath's ship's computer. But I don't want to get Rita's hopes up just yet. After so many years on a planet like that, it's impossible to know if her parents will still be alive when found.

"We don't have to go back to my small village for the wedding," Rita says. "There's a nice gathering space on board this ship." Each time she speaks, her breath tickles my neck and I'm tempted to forget about waiting until the wedding night and make love to her right now. But other than that night on

Aylvon, we haven't made love again, after we did research on the wedding traditions of our parents and found out that we are supposed to wait until the wedding night.

"That's your home," I say to Rita, trying to distract myself from where my thoughts are heading.

"Wherever you are, Bryn, is my home," Rita replies, snuggling up closer to me. "It just makes me feel sad when I think about how lonely I always was when I lived there. And now I'm heading back there. I don't know if the sisters will welcome me back or even want to see me."

I hug her tight, turning onto my side so I can pull her even closer. She wraps a leg around me. I want to tell her about our hope in finding her parents, but if I do, she'd want to go search for them herself, and the planet is full of blue crystal. It's not safe. There's also the possibility that Parrin and the others may only find the remains of her parents, which is something I never want her to see.

But if all goes as planned and they find Rita's parents, then the perfect place for us to get married, and for her to be reunited with her parents, is her hometown; the place where she'd waited for their return for so long.

Rita pulls herself up onto her elbow and looks down at me. "I still can't believe we have nothing more to worry about than just what we're going to wear to our wedding." She smiles and I smile back.

"I'm going to need some time getting used to being..." I try to think of the right word.

"Common?" Rita offers.

"Yes."

She kisses my cheek and lays on top of me. I sigh. Nothing has ever felt as good as this moment.

"You could never just be common, Takano Bryn Sanyn," Rita says.

I laugh at the combination of names.

"Nor could you," I say. "Rita Bryn Sanyn."

She leans forward, kissing me gently on the lips.

The bleep of the doorbell indicator startles the both of us. Rita jumps off of me.

"Who could that be so late?" She scurries off the bed.

"Wait," I say, but it's too late, she's already at the door. It slides open and Parrin stands on the other side.

"Parrin!" she says. "What are you doing here?"

"Uh..." Parrin says, his eyes traveling down to her night clothes. "Is Takano, I mean Bryn here? He wasn't in his quarters. I have some good news for him about our... diplomatic mission."

"Oh," Rita turns to look back at me, then back to Parrin again with a sigh. "Couldn't it wait until morning?" She sounds annoyed at Parrin and it makes me smile.

Parrin nods. "Yes, sorry. Just let him know that the diplomatic team is back and we were successful in our... negotiations."

"Okay." Rita steps back to let the door slide closed. "We'll see you at breakfast. I'm glad you're back safe."

Parrin nods and the door slides closed.

I swallow hard. Rita's parents are alive... and they are going to be at our wedding.

THE KEEPERS OF THE PEACE

"**Y**OUR DAD WANTS YOU to look over the guest list," Parrin says to me over the hum of our vehicles.

"Why?" I ask. "I won't know anyone on it." I look ahead, across the hot tundra. "Are you sure this is where the Temple Worshipers are?" I stop my speeder vehicle and jump off.

Parrin stops his speeder too and gets off as well. He removes his head covering, looking a lot more overheated than I am. The burns on his neck from the crystal beam exposure on Antineon still haven't completely healed yet and it reminds me of how near we came to losing our lives.

"I think your dad wants you to look over the list of names to see if you recognize any as from the Ruling Order," Parrin says, pulling out his small port reader. "RSVP is through military identification passport codes only," he continues. "News of your wedding is getting around fast and people are flying in from all over, wanting to attend. We don't want the wrong people to show up."

I sigh. "I thought it was supposed to be a small event."

"It is." Parrin hands me the port reader. "Here's the short list. But the announcement was public, so anyone could RSVP. They just need to be approved."

I remove my head covering and glance at the names. Most of the names I don't recognize. Even the droids are listed: Beeps, JoyBot367...

"Looks fine to me." I hand Parrin back his reader and take off my robe to let my skin breathe. The coulees drop down into steeper canyons. There will be some shade down below. It's the height of the summer season and this remote area, far south of Rita's village, is a lot hotter than the Northern forests where I first met her.

I head towards the canyons and look over the edge. The jump down to the bottom is a bit far, but I can slow my fall using my Gift abilities. I turn to Parrin.

"I'll wait up here," he says, looking down.

"Good idea."

I jump, landing with a soft thud at the bottom. The air is instantly cooler in the shade of the steep coulee.

The sound of trickling water bounces off the cliff walls around me. My arms, burnt from too much sun exposure, are now soothed by the cool air and shade. Parrin warned me to cover up this morning but the sun wasn't hot yet when we set out for the Southern regions to find the Church of the Gifted, in search of a Master to preside at our ceremony.

"We've been expecting you." A man in a Master's robe emerges from the shadows. He removes his hood revealing a head of silver gray hair. It reminds me of Master Kra'an.

"I came to find a Gifted Master," I say, unsure how to respond to his greeting. "We wish to have one preside at a wedding ceremony," I say.

"The Masters from the Church of the Gifted don't seal marriages," he replies.

I had already guessed as much, but Dad wanted us to come, possibly to keep us busy while he and Rita went off planet. They left to find a trading outpost known for its many fabrics and decorations for special events.

The decorations don't really matter to Rita. The real reason for the trip was to keep her away while her parents recuperate from their long journey and from their exposure to the blue crystal planet. They've regained a lot of their strength since undergoing treatments by Opposition doctors, but I haven't seen them yet.

Their presence makes me all the more anxious about the wedding.

Dukath's words still haunt me from the grave. Did I really spoil Rita's heritage as a princess by just being who I am, or who I once was? What if her parents don't approve of our marriage? I don't even think they know why they're on planet, other than being rescued.

"Thank you for your time," I say to the Master. I bow, hoping my disappointment doesn't show. It was a half-day's trip here and for nothing. "I'm aware of the Temple code forbidding two Gift Sensitive persons to be united in marriage."

"We will, however..." the Master says, "make an exception for the Keepers of the Peace."

I stand up straight. Is he talking about Rita and me?

"In your case," the Master continues, "the union has been written in the stars. The one who destroys the Supreme Leader of the Ruling Order, and the other who rises from the dead once he is destroyed; these two together will be the new Keepers of the Peace in the galaxy. I've seen the scrolls with the prophecy, myself. I am well aware of who you are Master Bryn Sanyn."

His words fill me with peace. "Then you will come to the ceremony?"

The old Master nods. "I will."

"The wedding will be in a few days. We will send a shuttle—"

"No need. I will start my pilgrimage to the celebration soon. I have waited long for this day. A privilege and an honor it is to me. You have fought great battles, faced great dangers and won victories both in the galaxy and within your own souls. You will continue to uphold the balance that is needed. Master Bryn, you have proven worthy of the one who is soon to rise to her destiny."

I am at a loss for words. I watch as the Temple Master walks away, back into the shadows from where he came.

This is really going to happen.

Rita and I are getting married.

are you ready?

I LOOSEN THE COLLAR of my uniform and peek out from behind the front curtain of the Preparations Tent. The sun is finally beginning to set, but it isn't the heat from the sun that is making me sweat. It's the thought of the wedding night. And before that, meeting Rita's parents for the first time.

She doesn't know they're here. It is going to be a surprise. Yet, now I'm second guessing the decision to have her see them for the first time, at our wedding.

The guests sit on chairs set beneath flowing tents of silk fabric, all dressed in the fine clothes of their cultures, waiting for the wedding to start.

This would be easier if I were allowed to see Rita. I'd been eagerly awaiting her return from the trading post planet, so I could finally see her again, if only just to remind myself that she really does want to marry me. But then I was told I couldn't see her until the wedding day.

I pace the small area inside the tent. Rita's late. What if she's flown off with Parrin on a small spacecraft, instead of going through with this wedding ceremony? She's had some time away from me now, to clear her head and think about it. She could have changed her mind.

"Master T'hakud is finally here." Dad barges into the tent, almost running into me. "Oh, Bryn. Why are you standing right at the entrance?" He smiles. "You won't see Rita out there, not until everyone is in place and seated. Are you ready?"

"Where's Parrin?" I ask.

"He's making sure everything is in order with the security fleet that's in orbit above planet. Had I known you were going to ask him to be your Best Man I would have appointed someone else as the Security Operations Commander for this important event."

"No one else is more fitting for Security Commander, than Parrin," I say, smiling at my dad. "He saved my life more than once."

Dad pats me on the shoulder. "You look wonderful, Bryn. And very nervous. Are you going to be alright?"

I nod.

"Do you have the ring?"

I nod again.

Dad gives me a hug, surprising me.

"I'm proud of you," he grunts, then lets me go. "And of Rita too, with all you've been through." He sets his shoulders straight and lifts his chin. "We traded a Combat Fighter Plane and an old B-Class Starfighter for a luxury shuttlecraft, for you and Rita."

"Why? We can just live on the Starship."

"This is for traveling," Dad says. "Just the two of you, not a whole fleet. You can go on a trip and have a little time to enjoy being married, before Randon assembles his forces and reboots that super weapon. Who knows what else he'll think of next."

"He's powerless without Dukath," I say, with more confidence than I feel.

Dad smooths out his tie. "It's your wedding day and I hope you'll enjoy your union for as long as you can. You should take time away to enjoy it."

I close my eyes for a second, imagining the sheer joy of spending even one full day relaxing with Rita and not worrying about anything else.

"She'll want to stay with her parents," I say, the image of us on a vacation suddenly slips away.

"Perhaps for a bit," Dad says. "But they do have to sleep at night. You two can at least have the luxury of being in a comfortable spacecraft for a little privacy, even if it's still on planet."

"Thanks, Dad."

A flute begins to play a lively melody outside the tent and my heart speeds up.

"That's our cue!" Dad opens the curtains. "Are you ready?"

THE WEDDING

I LOOK OUT OVER at the crowd but all I see is Rita. She's wearing a flowing white gown with gold accents and yellow flowers on it. She matches the rays of sunshine setting on the horizon behind her.

Her blonde hair frames her pretty face, surprisingly not pinned up for the occasion. But I may have told her I prefer the wild, carefree flow of her curls. She smiles and I smile back. A lump is already forming in my throat. She looks happy, even with the tears glistening in her eyes. And I'm happy too. So much so that it hurts.

Murmurs spread through the crowd as the guests turn to see Rita entering at the back of the celebration tent.

Beeps rolls towards the front, moving slowly down the aisle between the rows of chairs, dropping small, white petals of flowers onto the narrow purple carpet. She makes her way to the platform where me, Dad and Master T'hakud are standing.

The flute player stops and the string instruments begin a new song, one that's both sad and happy in its melody.

Everyone stands and turns to face Rita.

She walks forward, following after Beeps, but going slower. She looks only at me as she makes her way to the front. I know her parents are in the crowd, but she doesn't. Her mom didn't want to interfere with the wedding and asked to leave the surprise of their return until after the vows.

Rita's father is still too weak to stand for very long, although the tradition is for the father to walk the daughter down the aisle. Dad wanted to tell Rita before the wedding, but Rita's parents insisted.

I glance to the front row. Rita's mother is facing away from me now, watching Rita walk down the aisle, but I can see their similarities, even in the way she stands. Her father's shoulders are slumped and he wipes at his eyes.

My gaze returns to Rita and my eyes begin to burn with unshed tears. She glides down the aisle towards me. Her dad pulls her mom into an embrace as she passes by but Rita's eyes are only on me.

Parrin appears, looking a bit frazzled but still cleaned up, wearing a dark brown suit and his hair styled back. He's still wearing his commander's belt, showing beneath his suit jacket;

a comm device and a small blaster at the ready. He hurries to the front to help Beeps up onto the platform.

She rolls to the other side to stand beside Dad, while Parrin joins me.

He made it to the wedding after all. I guess there were no threats of unwelcomed guests trying to fly into the atmosphere.

Master T'hakud opens his arms in invitation to Rita as she steps onto the platform to stand beside me.

The music stops and Rita takes my hand. Her touch soothes me and my shoulders instantly relax.

"Welcome guests and family," Master T'hakud begins. He nods to Rita's parents and my heart pounds. I squeeze Rita's hand.

"We are gathered here today," Master T'hakud continues, addressing the crowd. "To witness the sacred union of Bryn Sanyn and Rita..." he pauses.

There is a moment of silence and hushed whispers. The tent's fabric flaps in the gentle breeze as everyone waits for Master T'hakud to continue.

It takes me a moment to realize he doesn't know Rita's full name and is waiting for someone to offer it.

Rita looks down at our hands, blinking back tears. She doesn't know her last name, either. The sisters never told her. I frown, remembering how they didn't give us permission to enter the temple where she grew up in, when we arrived, let alone have our ceremony there. They were afraid of Rita's new powers, and they didn't trust me.

"Gowron," Rita's mother says. All heads turn to her. "Rita Rue Gowron."

Rita glances over as well, her eyes searching the crowd for the person speaking. Then she lets out a small gasp.

"... Mom?" Rita's hands slip from mine. "Dad?" Her shoulders begin to shake and she looks ready to collapse. I reach out, ready to catch her.

Her mom and dad step forward and I can tell they're still weak as they try to get up onto the platform.

I put out my hand to steady them with my Gift energy, my vision blurred with tears. They both hurry to Rita and hug her. She falls to her knees and so do her parents. I step back to give them room.

Rita's muffled sobs tear at my heart.

Her mom lifts a tear streaked face and looks up at me. She takes my hand and I feel her Gift energy, strong despite her weak grasp. So she's the one who passed her Gift down to Rita, not her father.

She tugs on my hand and I get down on my knees with them. They pull me into their hug. Master T'hakud doesn't have to say the vows for us to know that we're a family now.

Never Again Alone

A CHEER ERUPTS AS Rita and I slice down into the elegant wedding cake with a large knife. Her hand is over mine and she presses down, getting cake icing onto my finger.

I smile. Most of her sparkly make-up has come off, after all the crying during the ceremony and now the leftover traces glisten on her cheek by the light of many candles and torches.

The dining and dancing is finally at an end, which is a relief since I don't dance. Rita's parents have returned to the medical clinic, as per doctor's orders, and couldn't stay for the cake cutting, but I'm selfishly glad I have her to myself now.

I study Rita's face. She looks tired, but happy.

Beeps rolls around our feet, recording holographic images of us cutting the first slice of our wedding cake.

"Oops, I got icing on your finger," Rita says, with a look of mischief on her flushed face.

We step away from the cake and the crew's chef takes over where we left off, cutting more pieces to distribute to the guests.

"It's fine." I lift my hand to lick off the icing, but Rita stops me. She takes my finger and does it for me. Heat washes over me at the feel of her lips on my finger, and I clear my throat.

Rita, stop. I gently my hand away and I kiss her on the lips, wishing we were alone.

"I don't feel like eating cake," she says. The look she gives me makes my stomach do a somersault.

"You don't like the cake?" the chef asks, turning to us.

"We love it," I say.

I scoop Rita up into my arms. I can't stand it any longer. I need to be alone with her. She squeals and pushes against me playfully but I ignore her protests.

"Thank you, again," I call over my shoulder to the chef. I hurry through the crowd, carrying my kicking bride.

"What are you doing?" Rita laughs.

I don't slow my pace, in case anyone tries to stop us to talk.

"My fancy shoes fell off!" Rita gasps. "We have to go back and get them."

"You won't be needing your shoes," I reply.

"Where are you taking me?"

I walk past the musicians on the small stage and the dancers providing entertainment. I can't see Dad anywhere but I'm sure he'd understand if Rita and I left the party early.

"What about the guests?" Rita says, looking back over my shoulder as we leave the torch lights behind us. We step into the glow of the moons resting on the hills.

"You started it," I say to Rita. "Now I want to be alone with you."

She hugs my neck tight and shifts her small frame in my arms until she has her legs wrapped around my waist.

"Bryn?"

"Yes?"

"Thank you."

"For what?"

Rita rests her head on my shoulder as I carry her like a little girl; the same little girl who once looked up at these very stars each night, unable to sleep as she waited for her parents to return. Only now, she's grown into a beautiful woman, one who will never feel lonely again.

She doesn't answer my question and I can't begin to guess all that she's feeling at the moment, with her life changing so drastically all in one day, getting married and finding her parents after so many years.

"I love you," I whisper to her as we approach our honeymoon spacecraft.

"I love you, too," she whispers back.

EPILOGUE (RITA)

I, RITA RUE GOWRON, having discovered that I am highly Gifted, of Royal blood and capable of murder as well as of falling in love, have now been reunited once again with my parents after many years.

Having aided in the destruction of the most evil Supreme Leader of the Ruling Order, Dukath, I too, died in the waters of Antineon, only to rise again to life and find my way back to my home planet, where I am now being carried in the arms of a former Dark Master, Takano Rynn, the man I fell in love with even when he was still an evil Master.

It's enough to make any girl dizzy!

The door to the bed chamber slides open with a gentle hiss and the sweet smell of flowers greets us from within. Takano carries me across the doorway into a luxurious room lit with tiny lights which give off a dim glow, like candlelight.

"Oh, it's beautiful!" I wiggle out of Takano's arms and head over to the bed that is covered in flower petals. "Oh no." I pick up a handful of the petals. "What happened to the flowers? Who would have destroyed them like this? Is someone sending us a threatening message?"

Takano takes a petal from my hand. "I think it's for decoration."

The petals are smooth cool to the touch. "I suppose they would feel lovely to lie on..." I say softly.

Takano's eyes glisten with what I can only imagine to be thoughts of me lying in this bed covered in these flower petals. But I don't want to read his mind at the moment, or else things will escalate far too quickly.

I walk over to the small door leading into the bathroom area and it slides open. The inside is twice as large as the facilities available in standard ship quarters, and the bath tub takes up half the space, large enough for even Takano to fit in comfortably. On the floor I see my bag of clothes. So they did deliver it for me. Good.

I turn and give Takano a tiny wave. "Give me a moment. I'm going to put on something a little more comfortable." I push the button for the door and it slides shut.

I hurry to my bag and open it. At the top is the long, sheer scarf I found at the trading outpost a few days ago. It's as light as the wind and about as see-through; not much to cover up with, but that's the whole point.

I slip my wedding gown off my shoulders and it lands in a heap on the floor. I step over the many layers of fabric and set the dress on the side of the bath tub.

My knees feel weak as I remove the rest of my undergarments. I'm hoping Takano will be pleasantly surprised. I'm already blushing at the thought of his reaction.

I catch a glimpse of myself in the full length mirror beside the sink. I don't recall ever seeing myself this way, fully reflected in a mirror while completely undressed. The first thing I notice are the talon scars of the great eagle on my shoulders, a tribute to the majestic bird's sacrifice the day I died on Antineon. He gave me a chance to remain in his body, in spirit, until I could return to my own again. He died on that planet, with the efforts of saving me.

I touch the scars, never wanting them to disappear; never wanting to forget the great eagle of Antineon. I suddenly realize that Takano and I now have matching scars.

I tilt my head to the side, inspecting my short hair. It makes me look tougher somehow, yet still feminine. My neck is exposed, giving me a more elegant look. But I no longer have my beautiful, long hair, the outward sign of my devotion to the Temple. The absence of it makes me feel tainted somehow. It was one of the reasons I wasn't allowed back into the temple when we arrived here, among many. Although, I wasn't surprised.

Takano's words come back to me, giving me strength. *No one is holy*. I may not fit the definition of holiness prescribed by the temple where I grew up in, but I have a Gift and a calling, and I have my family back now.

I close my eyes for a moment and say a silent mantra of gratitude; for second chances and for the blessing of being able to love someone, and being loved in return.

My eyes travel down to my ribs. Am I too skinny to be alluring? I glance at my thighs which are shapely from all the running and jumping I seem to do on a regular basis. Then I turn to look at my backside.

There's a knock on the door and I jump. "Just a moment!"

I grab the sheer fabric scarf and set it over my shoulders. It falls forward, over my chest, the fabric caressing my skin and making me shiver all over. I reach into my clothes bag for a belt then put it around my waist, setting the scarf in place. The patterns on it cover me just barely, still showing what's underneath. The effect is as alluring as I'd hoped it would be.

My reflection in the mirror makes me blush and my heart races with the anticipation of Takano's reaction when he sees it.

"Rita..." he says, his voice muffled from behind the door.

I take a final look at myself then walk over and press the open button quickly, before I get too nervous and change my mind.

The door slides open, creating a small gust of air which blows my scarf slightly.

Takano blinks in surprise. His gaze travels over me.

I step out of the bathroom and walk over to the bed. When I turn around again he's still standing by the bathroom door.

Will you join me? I hold out my arms to him.

He walks over and gets down on one knee so that he is no longer towering over me but looking up into my eyes. I smile, already wanting this night to last forever when it's only just begun.

Takano reaches his hand up and slides his palm over the back of my thigh. He tugs me gently forward and bends down to kiss my knee. Suddenly the room spins and I lose my balance.

Takano catches me in his arms before I drop to the ground.

"Rita?" He frowns. "Are you okay?"

"Is the shuttle moving?" I ask.

"No."

"I'm so dizzy..."

Takano's concerned look turns to a smug smile. "I guess I have quite the effect on you."

"No," I say, sitting up. "It's not that. I'm seriously dizzy... ouch!" A sharp pain hits my lower belly and I curl into a ball, hugging my knees and clenching my fists. "Ow, ow, ow."

"What is it?" Takano says, his concern returning. "I don't know." I shut my eyes tight against the stabbing pain.

Takano lifts me up into his arms. "Let's get you dressed. I'm taking you to the infirmary."

* * *

"Nothing to be concerned about," the medic announces, walking back into the room through a curtain. Easy for him to say. He's not the one who had knife jabbing pains in the stomach!

But now I'm feeling fine and have no pain at all, so I don't see why the tests couldn't have waited until morning.

My mom and dad stand on either side of me. They really should be resting and not worrying about some random pain I've had. Takano waits in the corner of the room, looking more worried than he needs to be.

It was nothing and I've made everyone worry for no reason.

"It's just as I thought," the medic continues. He sets his medical scanner down on the counter and gives me a smile. "Mrs. Rita Sanyn..."

"Yes?"

"Congratulations, you are with child."

ACKNOWLEDGEMENTS

I'd like to thank everyone who's encouraged me in writing this series, especially my fanfiction readers on Wattpad, without whom this series wouldn't exist!

Special thanks to Amanda Chomiak for her editing genius and Joan Mettauer for her keen eye for proofing. I'd like to thank The River Bottom Writers for being the place where I grew as a writer and in confidence, allowing me to take the steps I needed to become published.

Linda Penner, you inspire me and make me laugh, thanks for traveling these winding roads with me to making our dreams of becoming authors a reality.

Thank you to my husband Dave for his support and to my daughter Jessica for making brand new book covers for me!

Thanks to Elizabeth (aka Mom) for always believing in me and bragging about my novels at your work.

A shout out to my writing friends: Emily, Amber, Kaleen, Kirstie, Ian, Ken, Sandy, Leslie, Brock, Megan, Sarah, Shannon, Randy and the rest of you! (I'm sure there's a few I've missed, but I love you all). It's such a privilege to know so many awesome writers!

Please enjoy this special excerpt from
Book Three of the Rita Series
The Rise of Rynn (A Prequel)

THE RISE OF RYNN SYNOPSIS

BEFORE THEY WERE THE Keepers of the Peace, Rynn and Rita met and formed a bond which they long forgot about when they came face-to-face, on that fateful morning on Green Hill.

Previous to his reign as the mighty Takano Rynn, Bryn was a student in the Leadership Program of a new initiative called the Ruling Order, which aspired to one day rule the galaxy.

In order to be the ruthless leader he is expected to become, Bryn must conquer his emotions and commit to the Masters' Rule of no attachments. But will an unprecedented bond he forms with little Rue keep him from successfully completing the Program? Or will he succeed, with the help of unlikely friends Randon and Aurah, in facing the Ruling Order's Elimination Games as they struggle to cope with their forbidden attachments and their search for personal identity?

MASTER DUKATH

"**T**ODAY'S TEST," MASTER DUKATH says, "is to bring me the heart of a forest animal." He leans back in his chair and clasps his fingers together. His stare is unnerving, as always.

I frown. Each day the tests have been getting harder. Yesterday's was to make somebody cry. I don't enjoy making people cry, since it reminds me of when I would hurt people with my Gift powers and I didn't mean to.

Randon stands beside me, by far the most ruthless student in our Ruling Order training program. He succeeded in making someone cry on his way out of Master Dukath's study yesterday. It took him no time at all to accomplish the test. He told one of the child boarders at the school for the summer, that her parents died in a spacecraft malfunction on their way out of the planet's atmosphere. She ran away crying and calling for her grandfather, who is one of the instructors here.

I glance at Randon now. He has a stupid grin on his face and I imagine he's already planning some gruesome way to get the heart of an animal. All the tasks are easy for him. He has no conscience.

"Go ahead then," Grand Master says, dismissing us.

Randon turns and walks briskly out of the study, seeming eager to get started. I'm not as fast and get stopped at the door.

"Rynn," Grand Master says.

"Yes, Your Leadership?"

"Come and have a seat. I wanted to tell you this in private."

I walk back into the study and sit down, my heart pounding.

"Randon isn't ready to hear of this yet. He believes he is my favorite student," Grand Master says. "And I admit that I do find his enthusiasm... commendable. But he is not Gifted and doesn't possess any real power, like you do."

I nod, not sure what to say.

"Our new army, the Ruling Order, will be all powerful. You and Randon will rule the galaxy together, but you will be the leader."

I sit completely still. Did he say I would be the leader? I'm two years younger than everyone else in the program. Grand Master has always believed in me, when no one else did and when even my brother Morlin was beginning to give up on me. But Master Dukath told me he'd foreseen it, that I would become great and powerful if I joined him in building up the new Ruling Order.

"You have your grandfather's strength and Gift within you," Grand Master continues. "I will help you use it and you will become the most feared and most powerful ruler in the galaxy."

My chest fills with pride and it's hard to breathe.

"Your brother has taught you well," Grand Master nods and I frown. Morlin only held me back, always telling me to repress my emotions. But Grand Master encourages me to embrace my anger and rage.

"What are his thoughts on your returning to summer training?" Grand Master asks.

I shift in my seat. "I didn't tell him."

"Good. He would only discourage you. When he returns to find that you are the true leader that you were always meant to be, he will be ashamed for holding you back."

I stifle a smile. I don't want to seem too eager for praise, which would be unfitting for a future Master. But I'm still too young to be a leader, aren't I?

"I have high hopes for you my boy," Grand Master continues. "You will become a powerful, Dark Master."

"I will?"

"All in good time." Grand Master nods slowly, his eyes never leaving me. "Stay focused on your daily tasks. You must find your darkest emotions to truly become a Master, and I believe you will."

"Thank you, Your Leadership." I bow slightly then step back.

"And Rynn?"

"Yes, Your Leadership?"

"Tonight you are not permitted to sleep."

My chest deflates. "Am I being punished?"

"For asking me that, you will be, once I think of a suitable punishment."

My shoulders slump. I've said the wrong thing again.

"It's not a punishment, but to help you master your body and have greater self-control. In battle you don't sleep, for days, or even weeks at a time, not until there is victory. One night should be simple enough, even for you."

I nod. It's anything but simple, especially with how I feel the day after I get no sleep. For some reason Randon never has to do any of the self-mastery disciplines like staying up all night. Maybe Grand Master thinks he's already good at self-discipline. But I know there's nothing further from the truth. Randon lies and cheats and has no control over his temper or anything else that has to do with his emotions, or desires. I shiver at the last thought.

"Very well then, go on." Grand Master dismisses me with a small wave of his hand and I get up immediately. My head is still spinning with all that he's told me. Randon won't like it.

Now I have to go get the heart of a forest animal. I can't disappoint Grand Master. He's the only one who's ever believed in me.

THE LITTLE GIRL IN THE FOREST

I LOOK OVER MY shoulder to the school building in the distance. From here it simply looks like a pile of ancient ruins, abandoned at the end of an open field. The forest is dark and unforgiving, even in the daytime. Cool air wafts out from the dense trees which form a wall where the field ends and the forest begins.

I step over the thick roots of the old trees, heading into the forest. Above me the white clouds are obscured by gnarled branches and leaves. For a moment I wish I could fly—away from the daily tests and from Randon, and from Aurah the only girl on our summer training team.

She leans over the lunch table in front of me so I'll notice her breasts. I try not to look but I always do and I hate that it works every time. I'm not supposed to like girls or think about those kinds of things. Master Dukath says those things are for the weak and undisciplined, that Dark Masters don't allow such things into their minds or lives to distract them.

The wind rustles the leaves and I shiver. I came out here to find an animal but they all seem to be hiding, like they know I want their hearts.

"I can do all things through the Gift which strengthens me." I whisper the mantra my brother taught me as I walk through the trees. I can't tell if it actually helps to use the mantras but it's become a habit now.

A sound catches my attention and I stop walking to listen. It's coming from my left and sounds like a child crying. I head in that direction and see a little girl through the trees. She's kneeling in the dirt, mud on her light colored clothes. She's the same girl Radon made cry yesterday. She's holding something in her hands.

The leaves crunch beneath my boots and she looks over to me, her eyes wide and full of tears. I'm not supposed to talk to anyone outside of our summer training group, not even my mom over the comm unit. Not until the training is over. But I can't help but be curious about what the girl is holding. I'll just add this to the list of everything else I'm going to be in trouble for anyway.

"She fell out of her nest," the little girl says. Her voice has a high child-like pitch that I'm not used to hearing. I never had younger siblings, and I was taken out of regular schooling, early on.

"Can I see?" I ask.

She gets up and walks over to me. I step back, thinking she might accidentally touch me. I'm not allowed to touch anyone. When I do, Master Dukath seems to know instantly and I get punished for it. He says it will spoil my training and I'm to have no physical contact with others.

But he never seems to notice when Randon pushes me or hits me. That's also contact. But Randon is Grand Master's favorite student, or at least I thought he was, until today.

Am I really his favorite? He said I'd be a Dark Master someday and the leader of his new army, the Ruling Order.

"She's still alive!" The little girl holds up her hands to me and I see a tiny baby bird. I pick it up, careful not to touch her fingers as I do. The baby bird's tiny heartbeat flutters in my palm.

"My name's Rita-Rue," the girl says. "My grandfather calls me Rue. He lives here. I'm staying with him."

I watch the bird struggle in my hand and don't respond.

"How old are you?" the little girl asks.

"Fifteen."

"I'm five." Rue holds up her palm and spreads out five chubby fingers to show me the number.

"Oh, I thought you were like... three."

"I'm not three!" she yells. Her high pitched squeal makes me jump. I step back.

"I'm not supposed to be talking to you," I say, wrapping my fingers around the baby bird. I have what I came for and I should head back, before someone finds me talking to this five year old.

"I'm turning six soon you know," she says, clasping her hands behind her back and standing up on her toes. I nod and start to walk away.

"Wait!" she runs after me and grabs my cloak. "We have to put the baby bird back in its nest." She points up into the tree. I look up too, but I don't see the nest.

"I'm taking the bird," I say. There's no point in letting her think I would ever be her friend.

"Why?" she demands, putting her hands on her hips.

I frown. Usually kids are scared of me, like they can sense that I'm dangerous, but Rue is different.

"Because I have to take my Master the heart of a forest animal."

I look down at her round, little face, expecting her eyes to go wide with fear at what I've said. But she only nods, as though this is logical.

"Okay," she says. "The baby bird has a heart inside. You can take her to your Master." She crosses her arms. "But you have to bring her back when you're done and climb in the tree and put her back with her brothers and sisters after!" She purses her lips and tears fill her eyes. "You have to promise or give her back to me right now!"

"I promise," I say.

"Okay. But she'll miss her brothers and sisters. She'll be scared."

"She won't be scared. She's resting, see." I open my palm to show her the bird, then quickly close it again. "My hand is like a nest. She likes it."

Rue nods and wipes her eyes. "Okay. I have to go back to grandfather, but can I come play with you after lunch?"

"No," I say.

Rue's face turns red and my chest tightens. Is she going to cry or scream? I've never met anyone so emotional. Maybe if I lie to her she'll go away.

"I'll come find you after I put the baby bird back and then we can... play."

She smiles. "Okay. What's your name?"

I almost say Bryn, but stop myself. "It's Rynn."

Rynn's the new name I was given when I started training with Grand Master. And now everyone calls me Rynn. I just forget sometimes.

"Bye, Rynn." Rue runs off through the trees, like a little bird herself, her light frame moving fast. I'm tall and lanky and not a very good runner. I watch her go, wondering if she actually knows the way out of the forest, or if she'll just get lost deeper in it.

Should I follow her? The forest is scary at night and lots of people have seen the spirits of the dead Masters roaming about. They say if you look them in the eyes, you'll die.

I open my palm and look down at the baby bird, Rue's words still running through my mind. *She'll miss her brothers and sisters.* The bird's tiny heart still beats. I want it to live and I want to return it to the nest, like I said I would. But I won't.

I sigh, closing my hand again, then hurry back to the school.

Failure

I WALK INTO MASTER Dukath's study and Randon is already there. We're the only two who are part of the personal training with the Master. The other kids that are in the summer training for future commanders and leaders of the Ruling Order don't do the daily tests that we do.

I stop at the door, wondering if I should just wait until Randon leaves. I hate him. He always says something to make me look bad in front of Master Dukath, and sometimes he even makes stuff up. Then I sound stupid when I say it's not true, like I'm the one who's lying and trying to cover it up.

"Rynn," Grand Master says from inside the study.

I freeze.

"I know you're out there. Come and join us."

I step inside, the baby bird sweating in my hand now. Randon glances at me when I walk in. He has a stupid smirk on his face and his hands are all red with blood. He looks me up and down.

"Nothing to show for yourself, *Rynn?*" he says. "As usual?"

I ignore him and walk to Master Dukath's large wooden desk and set the bird down. It moves but has lost most of its energy, like a fish running out of air.

Master Dukath looks down at the sad, little creature and I can tell he's disappointed. I hold my breath.

"I asked for the heart, my dear boy, not the entire animal."

I don't answer and Grand Master looks up at me.

"You know all of these... creatures, are for our use, do you not?" he says. "They exist to help further a greater purpose, our purposes. Today it is for the purpose of your training, that this bird will be killed." He studies me a moment. "Do you feel sorry for the bird, Rynn?" he asks.

"No, Master."

"Then perhaps Randon could bring us a knife?"

My shoulders stiffen but I don't say anything. The bird moves again, trying to get up from its side but unable to. I close my eyes, angry at the little girl in the forest for making me promise to take it back. It just makes this harder. I'll tell her tomorrow that I killed it, and I'll make her cry, like Randon did. Then she'll leave me alone and not ask me to play with her anymore.

I hear Randon's hurried footsteps approaching from the hall and I open my eyes. How did he find a knife so quick? He's breathing fast when he walks in. Did he run? There's an evil grin on his face that makes my stomach tighten. He holds out a large kitchen knife to me. I take it and look at Master Dukath. He nods for me to continue.

"Don't be afraid," he says, putting his palms out. "Go ahead. The bird may be innocent, but sometimes we have to kill the innocent, to show those in power that we are serious and will use any means to achieve our goal. You will not be able to save the lives of many, if you cannot end the lives of a few. Go on. The bird's sacrifice is your growth in the powers of the Gift."

He's right. It's just a stupid, little bird. I clutch the knife handle, turning it in my hand. The bird is still alive. Why couldn't it have just died already, like a fish?

Suddenly Randon grabs the knife out of my hand and slams the blade down over the baby bird's neck.

"You lose," he whispers to me, then reaches in front of me for the bird. I turn away, unable to watch. I know what I should do. I should push Randon away and do it myself and get the heart, but I can't. I've failed again.

"You've failed again," Master Dukath says, echoing my thoughts.

I turn to face him. "And for that I know I will be punished," I say. It's the response I'm supposed to give if Grand Master says I've failed. I used to try and give explanations as to why I failed, but it doesn't matter. I know Grand Master approves more of this simple response, than anything else I'd have to say.

"For your punishment, you will stay out in the forest for the entire night. You must not sleep or even sit down, but wander deep into the forest and think about all the life around you, the life that is there to serve you, to serve all of us, feeding us and giving us air. We do not serve the creatures and plants, they serve us."

"Yes, Master," I say.

"You may both leave now."

Randon and I bow then walk out. I brace myself for Randon's ridicule, once we're in the hall. But he doesn't say anything and hurries ahead of me instead.

I frown. He's either in a really good mood or has something bad planned for me later.

I look down at my cloak. There are spots of blood on it from the bird. I don't care what Randon says. I haven't lost. I won't lose my chance at being a leader in the Ruling Order. I don't want to give him the satisfaction of taking that from me.

RANDON

THE FULL MOONS SHINE through the trees of the forest, casting ghostly shadows all around. My breath puffs out into the cold air and I pull my hood over my head to keep the chill away. I've spent the night roaming the forest before, as punishment. The first time was the worst and I had nightmares for days. But I never saw any ghosts, although I thought I heard them, and now I think I hear them again.

"I can do all things through the Gift, which strengthens me," I whisper. My words get lost in a gust of wind. A tree branch moves like the arms of a giant, with gnarly fingers silhouetted against the starry sky. I walk faster, heading for a clearing up ahead.

The snap of a branch behind me makes me stop. I turn, my adrenaline pumping. Visions of ghostly Masters with dark hoods and no faces invade my thoughts. But it's too dark in the trees to see anything.

Probably just a forest animal. I pull my hood lower over my head and keep going.

My boots crunch the leaves and branches as I hurry to the forest's edge. The tall trees sway wildly overhead and the wind lifts the leaves up around my feet.

Another branch snaps and I stop to listen.

Suddenly, a dark shape jumps out at me and I scream, falling to the ground. Two hands hold me down and I know by his familiar grasp that it's Randon. The roots of an old tree stab at my side, sending pain shooting up my back.

"Get off of me!" I yell, but my voice is drowned out in a rush of wind. Randon pins my legs down with his bony knees and his hands push on my wrists, making my fingers numb. My heart won't calm down, from the startle of his attack. "You're not supposed to touch me," I say.

"No, *you're* not supposed to touch anyone," he replies, sounding out of breath. "Because Master thinks you're so special. But you're not. And I can do whatever I want."

"Get off!"

Randon leans in close and I turn my head to the side. "I'm the only one that's ever going to want to come anywhere near you," he growls. "Even Aurah would never lay with you."

"I don't even want her to," I say, trying to push Randon off, but he's strong and two years older than me. My heart pounds wildly. I'm not allowed to use my Gift powers or I'll be expelled from the program. The tree roots dig further into my side and I clench my jaw.

"We need each other, Rynn," Randon says, his face close to mine.

I hold my breath, my stomach twisting. "I don't need you. I'm going to be like the Grand Masters who don't need anyone."

"Who said you could ever be a Grand Master?"

"Nobody," I say quickly.

"Well, you'll never be one. You're too much of a coward."

"Why don't you lay with Aurah?" I say. "She'll let you lay with her."

"She'll let anyone lay with her. I don't want Aurah. I'll get thrown out for unclean acts."

I stop struggling and give in, looking out past the trees at the stars in the distance. One day I'll be all powerful and I'll have armies and weapons and battle starships at my command. But for now I have to deal with Randon.

"Why won't you just leave me alone?" I say, defeated. "I failed another test. Isn't that good enough for you? You're passing them all."

Randon seems to consider this for a moment. "You'll never make it through the training course," he snarls, climbing off of me. "Have fun in the forest."

I sit up slowly, my back aching from the fall. Radon is already gone into the dark woods and I'm alone again, my body suddenly cold from his absence.

* * *

"What happened to you?" Aurah asks as I walk by her table in the dining hall. I try not to limp. I don't want to look even more pathetic than I already feel, for being sent out into the forest for the night. Randon's jump attack made me twist my ankle on some tree roots in the ground and now I'm hobbling when I walk.

I ignore Aurah and keep going.

After Randon's assault last night I walked as deep into the forest as I could, not caring about the ghosts anymore. I dared them to come and destroy me. I wouldn't have resisted. Randon's words got to me. I no longer felt sure I'd make it through the training, let alone become a Grand Master someday.

Early in the morning I reached the wide river and considered jumping into it, but the water wasn't deep enough for me to drown in so I came back here instead. Now I'm running late reporting back to Master Dukath and don't have time for breakfast.

"Where are you going?" Aurah calls after me. "Come and have breakfast with me."

I keep going to the next building, connected to the dining hall by a wide archway, leading to Master's study. The sun shines through the long windows, so bright that I feel like I'm walking in a dream, my mind hazy from lack of sleep.

Master Dukath isn't in his study when I get there.

I frown. I'll be in trouble when he returns, for being late. But at least I completed my punishment this time. I'll just have to wait here until he comes back.

There's a movement near the door and I stand up straighter, thinking it's Master Dukath. I look and see the little blond girl, Rue. She's got her hair in braids today and is wearing the same beige pants and a dust-colored shirt she had on yesterday, but now she has a towel hanging down her back, clasped at her neck. She stops when she sees me in the study.

"Did you fall out of the tree?" she asks, her eyes going wide.

"What tree?" I blink, squinting to see her. She's standing in front of the hallway windows with the sun shining so brightly behind her that it hurts to look at her.

"When you took the baby bird back," she says.

I quickly glance at the wooden desk, then let out a sigh of relief. It's cleaned of the bird's blood, and the bird is gone. I look back to Rue again. "If Master finds me talking to you I'll be in big trouble."

She nods then starts to walk away.

"Rue?" I say in a loud whisper.

"Yes?" she replies in an even louder whisper, looking back into the room.

"Why are you wearing a towel around your neck?"

She narrows her eyes at me in an angry glare. "It's my *cloak*," she growls, then stomps off loudly down the hall.

I hear new footsteps approaching and my heart speeds up. *Hurry Rue*. I can't afford any more mistakes. I'm starting to lose count of how many I will be punished for. What if Master Dukath regrets his decision to take me on as his personal apprentice? Randon says the only reason Grand Master tolerates me is because I have Gift abilities. But I know I can be a leader. I'm the youngest one here and everyone treats me like it. But when I'm older, it won't be that way.

Two elderly Masters walk by in the hall, their hoods hiding their faces. My shoulders relax when I see it's not Master Dukath. I'll have to stand here and wait for as long as it takes for him to return, if I can stay awake that long.

YOU SHOULD BE SCARED OF ME

I LIGHT A CANDLE and sit down on my bed. The smell of the sulfur and wax relaxes me. I stare at the flame. I used to miss the modern luxuries of home, but now I've gotten accustomed to the simple lifestyle of the Masters and I almost prefer it.

A breeze blows in through the partially open window, almost blowing out my candle. I look up at the picture of my mom on the dresser. I never did get a frame for it, but for some reason I brought it with me.

I close my eyes, feeling tired. Tonight I'm allowed to sleep, but I can't seem to. I thought I'd be so glad to finally get to bed, but every time I lay down I think of home and of Mom. I don't want to miss her. Her and Dad sent me away and now they expect me to come back on summer break, but I'm staying to do the leadership program. What's the point of going back? Just so they can look at me with pity when I lose control of my powers, then send me away again?

I get up and walk to my bookshelf to take down *The Book of The Masters*. Reading should help me fall asleep, or at least get my mind off of things.

There's a gentle knock on my door and my grip on the thick book tightens.

Please don't let it be Randon again.

I go to unlock the door. At least I won't be alone with my thoughts, even if it is Randon. I don't have the energy to hate anyone today. The hinges creek as I open the heavy, wooden door. At first I don't see anyone, then I look down at a head of blond hair.

"Hi," Rue says, tilting her head up and smiling. I frown.

"Where did you come from?"

"My home planet!" She sticks her chin up and gives me a defiant look.

I grin. "That's not very specific."

Rue seems to consider my words, but I can tell she doesn't understand. "Yes it is!" she finally replies. "My planet is *very* pacific."

"Shhh..." I kneel down to Rue's level. "You can't be here. I'll get in big trouble."

She shrugs, seeming unconcerned about me getting into trouble.

"Actually," I continue. "*You'll* get in big trouble."

Rue crosses her arms and still doesn't move.

"Rue," I give her my most serious look. "I'm training to be an evil Master. I do evil things, things you don't know about. I've always done evil things, like hurt people when I'm mad, even when I was only two years old. You should be scared of me."

Rue gives me a curious look but doesn't respond.

I frown. "I could hurt you," I say. "Or kill you by accident."

Rue uncrosses her arms and her hand comes up and smacks my cheek.

I blink in surprise.

Did she just slap me? Her tiny palm stays against my face.

I take her hand away.

"You can't touch me or you'll get into trouble."

Rue shrugs and I realize she doesn't care about getting into trouble.

"If you touch me you'll get really sick and die," I say.

Her eyes go wide and she shoves her palm in my face again. "Is that why you have the red spots on your face? Because you're sick? And you're going to die?"

"No!" I take her hand away again. "Don't touch my face, or my cloak, or my hands. And don't come to my roo—"

Rue squishes my nose with her palm.

"What about your nose? Can I touch your nose?"

"No." I push her hand away again. "I told you, I can be very mean, and scary."

"You're not scary."

"Yes, I am."

"No, you're not."

"If I get mad, I could kill you."

"No you won't."

"How do you know?"

Rue tilts her head to the side, as thought studying me. "Because I know. Mom says it's my gift. I can tell when people are nice inside or if they are evil inside."

I stare at her for a moment. A sound in the hall makes my heart speed up.

"You have to go now."

"Can I stay here? I'm scared in my room."

"No."

"But I can't sleep."

"Then stay awake, but do it in your own room."

"I want to stay here. I don't want to be alone."

"No Rue."

"Please?"

"It's against the rules."

"Everything is against the rules!" Rue yells.

"Shhh…" I grab her by the shoulders, then quickly let go. She's already made me break my vows.

"You're right," I say. "There are a lot of rules here."

"Why?"

A shadow moves in the torchlight down the hall. Someone is approaching. I hesitate a moment then quickly pull Rue into the room. I turn the handle all the way so it doesn't make a click sound when I push the door closed, then I slowly release the handle.

"If you get me into trouble I'll…" I turn to find Rue pulling out my grandfather's sword from under my bed. "Don't touch that!"

Rue jumps back, letting it go.

"It's mine!" I yell. "You can't just grab my stuff. It isn't yours!"

I push the sword back under the bed. Rue backs away from me until she hits the wall, then covers her face with her hands. I'm still on my knees, having tucked the staff safely back under my bed, and I wait to see what she'll do next. She crouches down and hugs her knees, then she begins to sob.

I groan. "I told you I would hurt you," I say, feeling bad but not wanting her to know that. "Just go back to your room."

"I'm sorry I touched your toy," she says, her voice muffled in her knees.

"It's not a toy."

She keeps crying and I suddenly feel very tired. "Please just go. I want to sleep."

"I want to sleep too," Rue says lifting her head. Her face is streaked with tears. "I can't sleep in my room, it's dark and scary and cold and I can't light the candles by myself." Her bottom lip quivers.

"Why do you cry so much?" I say, trying to sound angry so she won't feel sorry for herself.

"I don't know," she says, crying even more, only now she isn't covering her face and seeing her cry makes me feel like crying. I go over to her and sit down beside her, leaning back against the wall.

"Just... stop crying, okay?" I say.

She takes a few deep breaths and looks at me.

"I just cry at night time, because I always think of my mom and dad." She hiccups, then continues. "In the daytime I forget about home. I can look at the plants and bugs, and play with Mr. Rock... Oh no!" She screams her last words and I jump away from her in surprise. "Mr. Rock! I have to get Mr. Rock! He's going to be so scared! I forgot Mr. Rock!"

"Shhh..." I put my hand over her mouth to stop her from yelling but my palm covers her entire face and she freezes in surprise. I take my hand away and wipe the tears on my palm onto my cloak.

"We have to go get—"

I cover her face again. "Can you stop yelling?" I whisper.

She giggles against my palm and I pull my hand away.

She takes two breaths then yells, "we have to get Mr.—"

I cover her face, but I know that she wants me to this time.

She laughs behind my palm.

"Let's stop yelling and be serious about Mr. Rock. Okay?"

"Okay," she mumbles behind my palm.

I let go slowly. "You should go back to your room and find him," I start to say, but Rue isn't paying attention. She grabs my hand and pushes my palm to her face again, puffing up her cheeks and blowing hard so it makes a funny sound.

She giggles again and this time I get up.

"Wait!" Rue grabs the front of my cloak, putting all her weight into pulling me down again. I land on my knees and she throws her skinny little arms around my neck, hugging me tight, her strength surprising me.

"Please can come get Mr. Rock? please, please—"

I try to peel her off of me, but she won't release her death grip on my neck.

"You can go back to you room and—"

"No, it's too scary! You have to come with me!"

"If I say yes, will you let go of me?" I ask.

Rue quickly releases me and runs to the door. "I'll show you the way. I know all the places in the school and I even drew a map. Oh, I'll show you my map! It's in my room, too."

"I'll walk you back to your room and you can be with Mr. Rock, okay?"

"And then will you stay, too?"

I hesitate. I should just tell her yes, even if I don't plan on staying, so she won't start whining again.

"Yes," I say.

Rue's face lights up. "Okay! Let's go!"

Excerpt copyright © 2018 by Bianca Rowena. Published by Bianca Watson Canada.

BIANCA ROWENA

Bianca Rowena was born in Transylvania and moved to Canada at age five. She studied Writing/Producing/Directing at the Southern Alberta Institute of Technology, in the Cinema/Television/Stage/Radio program. She now lives with her family in Southern Alberta.

Visit her online at www.biancarowena.com

www.ingramcontent.com/pod-product-compliance
Lightning Source LLC
Chambersburg PA
CBHW011321310726
48973CB00011B/3007